The Vanishing

A Mystery Story

Ethel Cook Eliot

Alpha Editions

This edition published in 2024

ISBN : 9789362923363

Design and Setting By
Alpha Editions
www.alphaedis.com
Email - info@alphaedis.com

Contents

CHAPTER I
GREAT AUNT KATHERINE COMMANDS

Two boys and a girl climbed down out of the bus from Middletown when it made its final stop in front of the summer hotel at the head of Broad Street. The boys, between them, were carrying the girl's books and a goodly number of their own, for they were returning from the last session of the school year. To-morrow summer holidays would begin. They nodded a friendly good-bye to the driver and started off up the steep little elm-roofed street that sloped directly up to Ashland College, an institution for girls, perched on the highest plateau of this hill town. The boys' father was a professor in that college and the girl's mother an instructor. But in spite of their privilege of living in the lap of learning these young people had to take a daily nine-mile bus ride down into the bigger village of Middletown if they themselves were to get college preparation.

The boys were twins. They were tall and spare, even for boys of sixteen, and seemed all angles. They had thick thatches of auburn hair, whimsical faces, and generous, clear-cut mouths. The girl was sturdy, slightly square in build, with brown, straight bobbed hair. The bobbed hair was parted at the side and brushed away in a wing from her forehead, and this gave her a boyish, ready look. Her eyes were hazel and very clear and confident in their level glance, but when she smiled, as she did often, they crinkled up into mere slits of eyes, because they were slightly narrow to begin with, and then she seemed oddly Puckish. Her mouth was wide and her lips rather full, but for all of that, because of its uptilted corners, it was really a very nice mouth. She trudged along now between her two friends, the corners of her mouth more uptilted than usual.

"Oh, I'm so glad it's vacation! At last!" she was saying. "Mother and I are going to have just the nicest summer. We're going to take long walks we never took, make a new vegetable garden, and eat almost every one of our meals out-of-doors when it isn't raining. We may even if it does rain! When will your tennis court be done?"

"We're going to get right at it to-morrow morning," Sam Hart, the twin on her left, answered. "It ought to be finished by the middle of July or sooner if they'll let us borrow the roller from the Hotel. Then if your mother is as patient as usual with us, we may be champions ourselves before the summer's over."

"She's crazy to play," Kate assured them. "But she says we must remember she hasn't touched a racket in years and that you have to keep in practice to be any good at tennis. It was seventeen years ago she won that cup at the Oakdale Country Club."

"She must have begun playing when she was in creepers," Sam exclaimed. "I thought it was a regular cup, a real and regular tournament affair."

"It was, of course. And she was nineteen, foolish."

"She's thirty-six now then." Lee did the arithmetic. "It's funny that, being so old as all that, she has always seemed just one of us. Where did you ever get such a mother, Kate?"

"Oh, I took my time about choosing," Kate answered, apparently seriously. "I didn't snatch at the first thing offered. I said 'better not have any mother at all than one who isn't magnificent.' So I kept my head and refused to consider anything commonplace. You know the result, gentlemen."

The boys did not bother to respond even with a laugh. They were used to Kate's nonsense.

But now in their climb up the steep elm-shaded street they had reached the college campus on the "Heights" and Professor Hart's house set into its corner.

"I'll take my books," Kate said. "Thanks for carrying 'em. If I do a lot of weeding in the court, perhaps it'll pay you a little for having been such good pack-horses for me all this year."

But Sam shook his head at the outstretched hands. "I'm coming on with you," he declared. "How about you, Lee?"

"Me, too," Lee responded. "Wait a second till I pitch these things on to the piazza."

But Kate protested. "No, don't. It's almost supper time. The bus was late. We'll be busy, Mother and I. Come after supper, instead, and help us decide where the new garden is to be. Perhaps mother will play Mah Jong with us."

There was nothing to do but agree when Kate took a dictatorial tone. The boys meekly gave a pile of books into her arms and turned in at their own walk.

Kate's mouth kept its uptilted corners as she went on alone, humming to herself and thinking pleasant thoughts. She skirted the forsaken campus a little way and then took a short-cut across its lawns. She knew that the last student had left to-day, and there would be no "grass police" to shoo her back to the paths.

"It's great having all the girls gone," she mused. "Now I shall have a little of Mother to myself again."

Kate was justified in her pleasure in the girls' departure, for those older girls did take an unconscionable amount of Katherine Marshall's time and thought. Of course, Katherine had to teach them, Kate realized—that was how she earned their living. But she did not understand why, outside of classroom hours, they need be always underfoot. Kate was proud of her mother's popularity, but often exasperated by it, too; for those older girls never by any chance paid any attention to Kate herself. They were polite, of course, but most perfunctorily; it was her mother they came to see and on her least word and motion they hung almost with bated breath. The truth was that these indifferent, superior girls, always present and never of any use to her, turned the college year for Katherine into a loneliness that even her mother scarcely realized.

There were the Hart boys, of course, always. But boys cannot take the place of a girl comrade. Kate's mother was all the girl comrade she had. That was why she had not let the boys come with her now. For once, she would be sure to find her mother alone, and the hour would take on, for Kate, something of the nature of a reunion.

The house she now approached, across the street from the campus to which it turned its low and vine-hung back, had formerly been a barn. The college had made it over for Kate's mother into a charming cottage which despite its turned back was still part of the college property. Kate found her mother sitting on the little garden bench at the side of the big double doors that had once been the carriage entrance and now stood open all spring and summer facing the hazy valley. Her cheek was resting on her hand and the expression in her eyes was a very far-away one, a farther away than the valley one. But she became very present when she heard Kate's step.

"Oh, Kate, I thought you would never come!" she exclaimed. "Read this letter." She picked it up from the bench beside her and handed it to Kate. "It's from your Great Aunt Katherine!"

"What! Again?"

Why Kate exclaimed "Again" would be hard to say, for within her memory Great Aunt Katherine had only written her mother once before, and that was all of two years ago! That letter had been to tell of the sudden death of a semi-relative, a woman of whom, until that time, Kate had never heard. Would this have news of another death? It must be something of importance that had wrung a second letter from Great Aunt Katherine.

Flinging her books on the grass, and following them herself to sit at her mother's feet, Kate opened the smooth, thick, creamy sheet and read:

MY DEAR KATHERINE:

I am asking you to send your daughter Katherine to spend the month of July with me here in my Oakdale house. Unexpected business in Boston is keeping me from my usual trip abroad this summer. I do not know whether I told you when acquainting you with Gloria's tragic death that her daughter was left without home or protection of any sort and that I proposed to take her in. But such was the case. Naturally, ever since, the child has been peculiarly lonely here in Oakdale. And now that she no longer has her day school in Boston to occupy her, the situation is a really trying one. It has occurred to me that Elsie and your Katherine are very nearly of an age, both fifteen, and that they might find themselves companionable. So I am asking you to forget old grievances, as I shall, and send your daughter to me for a month's visit. I shall plan parties and theatres and good times for them, and promise you that it will be every bit as gay as it was when you were a young girl here, and not too independent then to let your aunt give herself pleasure by planning for yours. I have looked up trains and find that by leaving Middletown at one o'clock, Katherine, with only one change, will arrive in the South Station in Boston at six-fifteen. I shall expect her on that train Saturday of this week, and Bertha, Elsie's maid, will meet her and bring her out here in time for dinner. If for any reason that is not a convenient train for Katherine to take, will you please wire me what time she *will* arrive? Sincerely, Aunt Katherine.

Kate looked up at her mother, dazed. "Just like that!" she exclaimed. "Does Great Aunt Katherine expect us to obey her just like that?"

Katherine was grave. "Yes, she has always done things like this. That's been the trouble. And when things don't go exactly as she has commanded that they should, she is at first unbelieving and then furious."

"Hm. And who is Elsie?"

"Elsie is Nick's little girl, and a sort of foster-niece to Aunt Katherine now, I suppose."

"It was Nick's wife who was killed in the automobile accident in France, wasn't it it? But why haven't you told me about her, about this Elsie? I've always wanted a cousin so, Mother!"

"Well, she isn't exactly a cousin, you know. But even so, if Nick and I hadn't quarrelled, if we had stayed as we were, in the course of things you would have known each other and perhaps have been very dear friends. It would have been natural."

"Oh, Mother—quarrels! When you are so lovely, how have people quarrelled with you so? It's a—*paradox*. Now don't say I've used the wrong word!—But here's more, more to the letter!"

Kate had turned the letter over and discovered a postscript on the back. Katherine, who had missed it, bent down, and they read it cheek to cheek.

P.S. I will add, for this will perhaps make your acceptance the quicker to come to, that Nicholas's name is never mentioned here, either by me or the servants, or even Elsie herself. So that end of things need cause you no anxiety. Elsie is a charming, well-mannered child.

That paragraph had not been intended for Kate's eyes. Katherine understood that at once, but it was all that she did understand about it. She frowned, puzzled.

"Notice how she says 'Make your acceptance quicker to come to'," Kate pointed out sharply. "She takes it for granted you'll come to it, apparently. If there is any question, it's only one of time. But why isn't Nick's name mentioned?"

Katherine shrugged. "I am afraid she must have quarrelled with him, too, just as she did with your father and me. But if that's so it must be terrible for both of them, since he owes her so much and she counted on him so to make up for Father and me and later you, Kate, and everything! How could he quarrel with her? Why, he should have put up with anything!"

Katherine's cheek was again on her hand. Her face was all puzzle. "And why should Elsie be lonely in Oakdale?" she went on aloud, but almost to herself now. "Oakdale is quite a gay little place, and I know very well there are plenty of young people there. Some of them are children of friends of mine, friends I haven't seen since I was married. Why, there are even the Denton children, just next door to Aunt Katherine's! It's all very mysterious, Elsie's being lonely."

But mystery where Great Aunt Katherine was concerned was no new thing to Kate. Whenever she thought about Aunt Katherine at all it was always to wonder. Why should her mother be estranged so entirely from her only living relative, this aunt for whom she had been named, and who had been a second mother to her after her own mother had died, when she was a very little girl? Kate could never understand that situation. Katherine was so peculiarly gentle and forgiving and lovable! How could any one stay angry with her?

Last year, when Kate was fourteen, Katherine had tried to explain things to her a little. She had said then that Great Aunt Katherine's money was the cause of the feud. Only it was not the usual trouble that money makes in families. It was not that Aunt Katherine was selfish or proud. It was—oh, absurdity—that she was over-generous! She expected to force her generosity on her family whether they wanted it or not. It had begun with Kate's Grandfather Frazier. He and Great Aunt Katherine were half-brother and sister. When Katherine was about Kate's age now, Grandfather Frazier had failed in business and the very same month Great Aunt Katherine had inherited a fortune from an uncle on her mother's side. Until that turn of fortune's wheel Aunt Katherine had been a school teacher living with her half-brother and giving her spare time to mothering her namesake niece. When she woke up one morning to find herself a wealthy—a very wealthy—woman, she immediately decreed that her brother should share the good fortune with her just as she had for so long shared his home with him and his child. But Grandfather Frazier's pride forbade him to acquiesce in that. The uncle was not his uncle, and it was not only his pride but his sense of propriety that influenced him in his firm decision not to accept one cent from Aunt Katherine. All that he would allow her to do to help his financial situation was to buy the house from him in which they were living so that with the money he might pay his debts. Thereafter he insisted that she was his landlady and he made a fetish until the month of his death of being on time with the absurdly small rent.

Aunt Katherine had built herself a large and mansionlike house on part of the land that went with her brother's little house. And since he distinctly limited her in the things she might do for his daughter, she adopted, suddenly and to every one's amazement, a poor young boy, with no background whatever, who had been brought up in a "Home," and who at the time of her discovering him was working in a factory. She prepared him herself for college, sent him to Harvard, and thrust him, almost head first, into the "younger set" in Oakdale. He had married Gloria, a beautiful young Bostonian but with no especial "connections." That was all that Kate knew of him, except for this late knowledge that he had a daughter.

Kate could understand her grandfather's pride, dimly. But her mother's case was not so clear to her, not quite. Her mother had married a rising young diplomat, a man of supposedly some wealth and assuredly fine ancestry. But on his death, not long after Kate's birth, it was discovered that there was not a cent to which the young widowed mother could lay claim. Katherine had never explained to Kate how this had happened. She hardly knew herself perhaps, because the processes of Wall Street were a maze to her. Almost gleefully, Aunt Katherine had seized upon this opportunity to offer her niece a home with her and a substantial allowance so that she might feel independent in that home. Katherine had refused point blank. And Aunt Katherine, now very sensitive on the subject of rejected generosities, had made a clean break with her namesake, washed her hands, and dropped her out of her life, much as one might drop a thistle that had pricked too unreasonably.

Katherine, determined to earn her own and her little daughter's way, had obtained an instructorship here at Ashland College, worked hard and happily ever since, and gloried in her independence.

The whole reason for this choice of poverty and hard work Katherine had not told Kate. But she had hinted that there was a very deep reason and one that justified her. Sometime, perhaps, she would disclose it. Meanwhile, Kate gave all this little thought, and was only brooding over it now because of the letter in her hand.

After a minute she said firmly, "If Great Aunt Katherine thinks I'm going to leave you here alone on this deserted hill-top for a whole month of our precious vacation, she has a surprise in store. Shall we write or wire our regrets, Mother?"

"We'd better write," Katherine answered, getting up suddenly and beginning in an unusually energetic way to pull up weeds from the lily-of-the-valley bed under the window. "I shall write that Saturday is too soon, for there must be some preparation on our part for such a visit. By next Tuesday, though, I should think you could be ready."

Kate turned her head to follow her mother with amazed eyes. "You don't mean I'm to go, Mother?"

"Yes, I want you to go. I want you very much to go. Aunt Katherine apparently needs you. I think, though, she must be drawing on her imagination a bit as to the loneliness of Oakdale for Elsie, especially since she herself says there will be parties and good times for you. You can't have parties without young people! Even so, her saying she needs you makes our acceptance not only dignified but imperative."

"But to leave you here alone! How could I ever do that? What are you thinking of?"

Katherine laughed at her daughter then. She was extraordinarily pretty when she laughed, startlingly pretty. But when she sobered, as she was bound to do too quickly, she was quite different, still lovely but not startling. Her face, sober, was intensely earnest. She had a rather square and strong chin but with wide, melting gray eyes to offset it. Her dark curly hair, which when undone came just to her shoulders, could be held in place at her neck with only a shell pin or two, it was so amenable in its curly crispness. Her cheeks and little slim hands were tanned, but with healthy colour showing through, making her, Kate often said, exactly the colour of a golden peach. She was slim and very graceful and not tall.

But in spite of all Katherine's loveliness and feminine charm, the impression one gained from her was one of over-earnestness, a fire of intense purpose steadily, even fiercely burning under the outwardly gay and light manner.

Now she was laughing. "Why shouldn't you leave me alone?" she asked. "And I won't be so alone, either. The Harts are staying. The boys will be my protectors and my playfellows both. I've been a fortunate woman all these years to have two such boys as well as my girl! And three mornings a week, you know, I shall be busy helping Mr. Hart with his cataloguing.... Now we shall have to collect all our wits and think about suitable clothes for you."

Kate's heart began to beat. When she had read the letter she had not let herself even contemplate what going would mean, not for an instant; for she had not dreamed her mother would so fall in with Aunt Katherine's plan. But since she had fallen in with it, since she wanted her to go—well, it was very exciting! For the first time she might have for a comrade a girl, a girl of her own age, a chum! For if Elsie, that stranger unheard of until a few minutes ago, was lonely, What was she, Kate Marshall? Oh, she would surely be gladder of Elsie than Elsie could possibly be of her!

She went to the border of the lily-of-the-valley bed and began weeding beside her mother.

"I don't see what we'll do about clothes," she said a little tremulously, not yet really believing in this new vista that seemed opening before her, like the valley there, at her very feet. "If I do go, I suppose Aunt Katherine will expect me to dress for breakfast and dinner and supper and in between times in that splendid house of hers."

"No, not quite so bad as that; but she certainly will want you to have—let's see—two ordinary gingham dresses, a little dinner frock, a party frock, a white dress for church, a sport coat and hat, a garden hat, a street hat, a street suit, a———"

But Kate interrupted this list with a quick laugh. "She'll want in vain, then. Let's get down to business and just discuss the must-be's, if I *am* to be a pig and go and leave you here alone for July with a vacation on your hands."

Katherine straightened up, brushing the soil from her fingers. Her quick ear had caught a joyous lilt in the voice and laugh that to an ordinary ear would have sounded merely dry. Her own heart leapt in sympathy with Kate's.

"Fortunately there's my pink organdie. That must do for dinners," the mother began, counting on her earth-stained fingers.

"Pardon, Mother darling, *my* pink organdie. It's been mine for over a year. Why will you go on calling things yours for years and years and years after they have descended? There's *my* pink organdie then. It'll have to do for church and for parties and for summer best just as it would if I were here. Two gingham dresses almost new. The blue flannel—but that will be too warm and scratchy for July, I'm afraid. Oh, Mother, that's just all. I simply can't go to Great Aunt Katherine's, and I'll never know Elsie!"

"Of course you can. Haven't we always found a way to do the things we really wanted? Wait a minute. There's my new white linen. I shall fix that for you. But your gingham dresses will never do, not for Oakdale. Never!"

"You're not to give your white linen to me. It's the prettiest thing you've got."

"Hush! It will make a charming street suit. It will need a black silk tie and a patent-leather belt. I can *see* you in it."

"You can, but you won't!" But when Kate saw her mother's dazed, puzzled little frown that invariably met her rare impertinences, she relented. "Oh, Mother," she cried, "if I'm to have your very best things added to mine, of course I shall be perfectly fixed. It will be a regular trousseau."

"I don't need anything but these old smocks, staying here," Katherine insisted. "And that's exactly what I shall do, give you everything of mine that can possibly be of any use. For once in your life you are going to have just an ordinary young girl good time. And if you and Elsie do hit it off, perhaps Aunt Katherine will consent to her coming back with you for the rest of the vacation. Come, let's spread all our possibilities out on the beds and see what there is!"

"Yes, after we've pared the potatoes for supper," Kate agreed, trying desperately to hold on to her last shreds of casualness and poise. "We had better have supper to-night, I suppose, whether I go to Great Aunt Katherine's or not. It must be six o'clock now."

Katherine threw an arm across Kate's shoulder as they went through the big door. "How fortunate it is," she said, not for the first time, "that I have such a steady, common-sensible little girl!"

But Kate would not abide her own hypocrisy.

"Oh, Mother, don't make me feel cheap!" she exclaimed. "You know perfectly well that I'm just bursting with excitement, only I'm ashamed to show it, for it's you who are going to be left at home doing just the same old things and seeing just the same old people and everything."

"But I'm happy doing just that," Katherine hurried to assure her. "Why, you yourself, Kate, have been looking forward to your vacation here and planning it with such pleasure!"

"Ye—es. But that was before this came. Now I don't see how I could bear the thought of just staying here! Now that I'm going to have pretty clothes and go to parties and meet some boys and girls, and have a girl chum of my own—why, what I was so looking forward to doesn't seem anything at all. I've suddenly waked up, and there's a big door open right in front of me, bigger than our funny old front door! I'm going through it, right into such fun! Only I'm leaving you behind. That isn't fair."

Katherine was quick to understand. Kate's whole mood was as real to her as though it were her own. She said, "But don't you see, dear, I *had* all that fun a thousand times over when I was a girl. Aunt Katherine gave me parties galore and took me to the theatre as often as Father would let her and there was anything worth seeing. And now that you are to have some of that life for a month, I am delighted. I only wish Aunt Katherine had asked you sooner. I have truly always hoped she would. Only, I suppose, she thought I was like Father and wouldn't accept things for you any more than for myself. And oh, Katie dear, do try to be patient with Aunt Katherine, no matter what she does or says! Perhaps you will make up a little to her for what I have taken away."

They stood now in the kitchen, facing each other. Suddenly Kate laughed, her nicest laugh that screwed up her eyes into slits and turned her into a Puck. "Let's put off supper then," she cried. "Stodgy old suppers we can have any night. Let's get out all the clothes we've got and just plan. I'm not going to let you touch any of your good ones for me. I'm truly not. But there may be some old things we've forgotten."

"Now you're really common-sensible, my dear," Katherine affirmed. "Before it was only pretend common-sensibleness."

And arm-in-arm, without one look at the kitchen clock which now was pointing to all of quarter past six, they went through the funny, merry little barn house toward the bedrooms.

CHAPTER II
THE BOY IN THE FLOWERY, DRAGONY PICTURE FRAME

During the next few days of hurried preparation for the visit the Hart boys found themselves almost entirely left out of the life in the little barn house, the house that ordinarily served as a second home for them.

"No time for boys to-day," Kate would call out crisply when they appeared at windows or door. "Woman's business is afoot. We're too busy even to look at you."

And Katherine, who was usually so much more easily beguiled and quick to see their side in any argument, for once echoed Kate and upheld her in her determination to stick to the tasks they had set themselves.

In spite of all Kate's protests, Katherine's new white linen was ripped to pieces and remade for the traveller into a jaunty street suit. With a black tie and narrow black patent-leather belt, when it was finished it looked as though it might have come from some fashionable shop in New York. Kate could not help being delighted. The pink organdie, which had done Kate duty for best all last summer, and Katherine for best for several summers before that, was now freshened with new lace and decorated with narrow black velvet ribbon. It was not only becoming, but quite up-to-date, and when it was finished and Kate surveyed herself in it in the glass, standing on a chair to see it all, they both decided that Kate would be able to put clothes definitely out of her mind when she was wearing it, for it was quite appropriate for all the occasions it was destined to grace.

And finally, Katherine's pretty bedroom was robbed of its month-old chintz curtains which, under her magic, in the space of two days only, became two simple but unique and pretty morning dresses for Kate. Now all that remained to be thought of in the way of clothes was the travelling suit.

"My navy blue silk will do perfectly," Kate said. "If I'm a little careful, it won't hurt it any, and next winter it will be as good as ever for your teas and things, Mother, unless I've quite grown out of it. Anyway, travelling won't spoil it."

When that was agreed upon it naturally followed that Katherine's new spring hat must go with it; for it was a little navy blue silk hat, light and small and quite fascinating.

"What you'll ever do for a hat I don't see," Kate worried.

"Never mind about me," Katherine told her nonchalantly. "Here on this hill-top anything does so long as it gives a shade. And if ever I go down to Middletown I can wear your black tam."

In the silk dress and hat and with her last spring's blue cape with its orange silk lining Kate felt prepared to meet the eyes of even Elsie's maid with equanimity. But imagine a girl of fifteen having a lady's maid!

Katherine thought that was just a glorified title for nurse, probably. But Kate protested that. A nurse for a girl of fifteen would be even more absurd than a maid. Well, Katherine was sure Aunt Katherine herself wouldn't have a maid. She was a New Englander with all a true New Englander's scorn of self-indulgence. But she probably did need someone to keep Elsie mended and possibly to be a sort of chaperon for her, too; for Aunt Katherine, since her inheritance, had interested herself in social and charitable work and was a very busy and even an important woman.

The two had endless conversations about Aunt Katherine and the adventures awaiting Kate. And Katherine talked more than she had ever talked before about her own girlhood in Oakdale and the little orchard house where she had always lived and where she had been so happy.

"If it isn't rented you must go into it," she told Kate. And then she described the rooms for her and all the important events that had happened in them. Aunt Katherine's big newer house she hardly spoke of at all, for Kate herself was so soon to see it and know all its corners.

All the planning and sewing and the long intimate conversations about Katherine's girlhood and bits of family history that Kate had never heard before, kept her right up to the eve of departure occupied and excited. But as bedtime approached that night she began to be shaken by unexpected qualms. She had never before been away from her mother for even one night and they had always *shared* adventure. That now she was actually to go off by herself into an adventure of her own seemed unnatural and almost impossible.

They were sitting on the bench out beside the big front doors, breathing in all the cool night air they could after the last hot and rather hurried day. Their faces were only palely visible to each other in the starlight. They had been silent for many minutes when Kate said suddenly, and a little huskily, "Mother, may I take the picture of the boy in the silver, flowery, dragony picture frame along to Oakdale with me to-morrow? He's a sort of talisman of mine."

Katherine was used to Kate's abruptnesses and seldom showed surprise at anything anyway. But now she did show surprise, and the voice that answered Kate quivered with more than surprise.

"The silvery, flowery, dragony picture frame? And the boy? What do you know of him, Kate?"

"Why, he's always been in the little top drawer of your desk. He's *always* been there. I've never told you how much he meant to me. I've made it a secret. But I've known him just about as long as I can remember. I was an awfully little girl and had to climb on to a chair at first to see him. But I didn't climb to look often. I saved it for—magic. When something dreadful happened, when I was punished or lessons were just too hateful, or you were late coming home, then I'd climb up and look at that boy in the frame for comfort. I think it would be very comfortable to have it with me along with your picture, Mother."

Katherine did not answer this for some time. She stayed as still as a graven image in the starlight. Finally, without moving at all, and in a voice as cool as starlight, she asked, "But why did you make it a secret? I don't understand a bit. I didn't know you even knew there was a little upper drawer. It's almost hidden, and there is a secret about the catch. You have to work it just so."

"Yes, I know. And I can't remember how or exactly when I discovered how to work it. At first, I do remember, it was just the frame I loved. It is a little wonder of a frame! The silver was so shining, and then the flowers and the fruit *and* the dragons are all so enchanting. I traced the dragons with my finger over and over and played they were alive. I thought it was too mysterious and lovely, all of it! It fascinated me in a way I could never tell you."

Katherine remained silent and Kate went on: "It was only when I was older I began to look at the picture and feel about that so strangely. I discovered what a wonderful face that boy has. I pretended he was the Sandman, the one who gave me my dreams at night. I always had such wonderful dreams, Mother! Remember?"

Katherine did not answer, and Kate felt somehow impelled to go on. She was surprising herself in this account of past childish imaginings. She had never thought about it in words like this before.

"He'd be just the person to have made those dreams for me. His face said he knew them all and thousands and thousands more! Then, when I got older I forgot about his being the Sandman, and anyway, my dreams stopped being wonderful and were just silly. Then I called him the 'Understander.' When I especially wanted an understander I'd open the secret drawer—I could do it without climbing on a chair by then—and there he was, looking up at me out of the dragons and the fruit and the flowers with *understanding*.

"It was all just a notion, of course. Oh, am I talking nonsense, Mother? And was it nonsense to keep it so secret and all, always?"

Katherine answered emphatically, "No. Not nonsense a bit. Only surprisingly—intuitive. For, Kate, he is just the sort of person who *could* have made up those wonderful dreams you used to have. And he was—and is still,

I suppose—just a perfect understander. That is his quality. And it is startling to me, all you have said, for he has been a sort of a talisman to me, too, all these years. I've looked at him, at the picture, when *I* needed understanding. And that is surprising in itself, for once, when he was just the age he is in that picture, the very week the picture was taken, I did him a wrong, a great wrong. We quarrelled. Since then I have never seen or heard from him."

Kate turned upon her mother with real exasperation at this disclosure. "Oh, Mother! How could you! Another quarrel!"

Katherine said nothing, and Kate instantly softened. She felt that she had wounded her mother; and that was a dreadful thing to have happened on this their last night! It was in an apologizing tone and humbly that she asked then, "And may I take him with me to-morrow?"

"No, I think you'd better not. Let him stay just where he is, in the secret drawer. I may need his magic more than you while you are away."

So her mother wasn't really hurt at all, or cross. She had spoken lightly, even airily. Kate sighed her relief. "I'm not asking you who the boy is, notice?" she spoke as lightly as her mother. "It might spoil the magic if I knew a human name for him. And I don't believe you ever did him a wrong, either. For one thing, I don't believe any one could do him a wrong. And you never did any one a wrong, anyway. I know it. You're too dear and kind.— Look at those fireflies out there. Watch me catch one!"

Kate suddenly jumped up and ran away into the summer evening. Katherine stayed still on the bench, watching her quick motions, her leaps and runs and turns. "It's very like a dance," she thought. "Only there should be music." And she began humming softly.

*　　*　　*　　*　　*　　*　　*　　*

Kate slept that night with the twinges of premature homesickness dulled by fatigue. And when morning came with the last bustle and scurry, any doubts that still lingered back in her mind were lost in the glamour of the adventure whose day had at last arrived.

"I'm going to take 'The King of the Fairies' with me to read on the train, Mother," she called from her bedroom where she was putting the very last things into her bag.

Katherine came to stand in the doorway, a partly spread piece of bread for a sandwich for Kate's luncheon in her hand. "But you know 'The King of the Fairies' by heart," she said. "Why not take the mystery story Sam and Lee gave you?"

"I've packed that. I believe you want 'The King of the Fairies' yourself, just as you want the picture!" Kate said, teasingly.

"Perhaps I do. It's without exception the nicest thing that has happened to us this year, I think. Bring it back safely, for I shall certainly read it again before the summer's through. Suppose we had been so foolish as to decide we couldn't afford it that day we stumbled on it in the bookshop and were lost at the first paragraph!"

Kate gasped at such a supposing. "I simply can't imagine having missed it, never read it, can you? If that had happened, well, everything would be different. It has made so many things different, hasn't it—reading it?"

"Yes, for us both, I think. That's why I am sure it is a great book, because it does make such a difference to you, having read it or not. And I understand your wanting it with you to-day. Try to get Aunt Katherine to read it, if you can. She has enough literary appreciation to realize its beauty, and the rest of it, what it does to you—well, it wouldn't hurt to have it do a little of that to her, too!"

At that minute Sam and Lee whistled from the road, out at the back of the house, and in a second they were around and in at the big front door calling for Kate's bag and anything that was to be carried. Katherine hurried to finish the sandwiches and tie up the lunch, Kate gave her hair a last boyish, brisk brushing, put on her hat, took her cape on her arm, and they were off, hurrying down to Broad Street and the bus there waiting the minute of starting in front of the Hotel.

"Don't let your father work Mother too hard on that old catalogue," Kate besought the boys. "And do write me sometimes about everything, the tennis court and all."

Sam and Lee promised that they would take turns writing, much as they disliked it, and Kate should not lack for news. "And bring Elsie back with you to repay us," they commanded. "The Hotel has let us borrow the roller, and the court will be in fine shape. We'll be all practised up, too. You'd better do some practising yourself while you're there. Elsie is probably a shark, anyway."

They reached the bus in good time and stood chattering a few minutes before the bus driver facetiously sang out, "All aboard!" Kate was the only passenger that morning. One quick hug and kiss passed between mother and daughter while Sam put in the suitcase and Lee dropped "The King of the Fairies" and the box of lunch in at the window. The busman himself had climbed into his seat and was sitting with his back to them. The Hotel piazza was deserted for the minute. There was no one besides themselves on the street. Sam kissed Kate on one cheek, and Lee kissed her on the other, quick, sound, affectionate, brotherly kisses. The driver blew his horn twice just to make sure no traveller was belated in the Hotel, started his engine, and the adventurer was off.

Kate stood in the little vestibule, hanging to the door and looking back as long as she could see the three people she was leaving. Katherine was between the boys, hatless, in a blue smocked dress; she was waving and blowing kisses. She looked like a sister to the boys, and not even an older sister from the distance of the speeding bus. Then the vehicle jerked around a corner and Kate sat down, faced about the way they were going, and contemplated her own immediate future.

In school she had often sat watching the big clock over the blackboard in the front of the room; just before the minute hand reached the hour it had a way of suddenly jerking itself ahead with a little click. That was what had happened on the instant of parting from her mother—time, somehow, or at least her place in time, had jerked suddenly and unexpectedly ahead. Now the hour must be striking, she reflected whimsically, and she was at the beginning of a new one. So much the better. She expected it to be a wholly fascinating hour, and Elsie the unknown comrade was waiting in it.

CHAPTER III
THE COMRADE DOES NOT APPEAR

Although Kate kept her book "The King of the Fairies" on her lap in bus and trains, she did not look into its pages at all. Still it had its meaning and its use on the journey. It was something well known and dearly loved going with her into strangeness and uncertainty. Its purple cloth binding spoke to her through the tail of her eye even when she was most busy taking in the fleeting landscape. One would have thought her a seasoned traveller and a very well-poised person if he had seen her sitting so still, her hands lightly touching the closed book, her gaze missing little of interest in country and town as the train rushed along. But in reality her mind was as busy as the spinning wheels, and her thoughts ranged everywhere from the commonplace to the inspired; and as for her emotions, they were in a whir.

But the thought that recurred over and over and from which she never entirely escaped during the whole five hours of travel was this: was any one else in the world so happy and elated as she? People she saw looking from windows, people working in factories, people working in meadows, people walking on streets—how dull and uneventful their present hour was compared to her present hour! And the Hart boys back at home! How could they bear the commonplaceness of going on in the same spot all summer, doing the same things, and seeing the same people! And only one week ago she herself had been more than contented, happily expectant even, when she was facing just such a summer!

Of course, she wondered about Elsie a lot. In fact, she scarcely thought of Great Aunt Katherine at all. Would Elsie meet her at the South Station in Boston? Great Aunt Katherine's letter had said Elsie's maid would meet her. But surely Elsie herself would be there, too. Kate, for a minute, imagined herself in Elsie's place, eagerly waiting among the crowds at the great terminal for the appearance of the new friend, wondering and speculating about her, just as Kate herself was wondering and speculating about Elsie.

The journey seemed very short. Kate could not believe they were actually in Boston until the conductor coming through assured her that in less than two minutes they would be in. But for Kate the next two minutes seemed longer than all the rest of the journey put together. She sat on the edge of the seat, one hand grasping the handle of her suitcase, the other clutching "The King of the Fairies." And even in her tense excitement the long-drawn-outness of those two minutes made her think about the King of the Fairies and what he had taught, or rather shown, the girl and boy in the book about *time*—what a mysterious thing it was, quite man-made and not real. She could well believe it now. However, even that two minutes came to an end, as such eternities will.

At the train steps there were "red caps" galore clamouring for baggage to carry, and a pushing crowd of passengers who had poured down from the long line of coaches. Kate shook her head as a matter of course to the porters, and marched along, her rather heavy leather bag, marked with the initials K. M. in white chalk, in one hand, the book and her purse—not a very good balance—in the other. No one could come out into the train shed to meet you, Kate remembered now from the two or three times she had been in that station with her mother. Well, Elsie would be up at the entrance, standing on tiptoes, looking off over heads until their eyes met. How should they know each other? No special arrangement had been made to insure Kate's being recognized. But Katherine had said, "Don't worry. Aunt Katherine's not one to bungle anything. She or Elsie or the maid, probably all three, will spot you at once. And if they don't, all you have to do is to find a telephone booth and call up the Oakdale house." And now, coming up through the shed, straining her eyes toward the gate, Kate had not the slightest doubt that the minute her eyes met Elsie's eyes they would know each other. She had lived in anticipation of this minute now so steadily for so long that she would feel confident of picking Elsie out in a crowd of a thousand girls all of the same age.

But she was getting near the gate and still she had seen no one that might be Elsie. Then, walking on tiptoes for a second, a difficult feat when you are as loaded down as she was, she did see a girl standing a little way back from the gate and watching the passengers with impatient eagerness as they came through. For an instant the eyes of the two girls met. Kate went suddenly, unexpectedly shy at that encounter. But instantly an inner Kate squared her shoulders, in a way the inner Kate had, and forbade the outer Kate to tremble. And when Kate, in a flash, had restored herself to herself, she knew that the girl waiting there was certainly not Elsie; she was too utterly different from anything she had imagined about her. There! She was right. The girl had greeted the woman just ahead of Kate and they hurried off together talking volubly. Kate drew a relieved sigh. She never could have liked that overdressed girl as well as she knew she was going to like Elsie. They would never have become chums and comrades.

But now she herself was outside the gate. She suddenly realized that her suitcase was very heavy and put it down. Simultaneously she looked around confidently for a friendly, welcoming face, for the eyes of the new comrade. There was no such face, no such eyes. But she did become aware of a youngish woman, in a very smart gray tailored suit and Parisian looking black hat with a gray wing, bearing directly down upon her. She was certainly too young to be Great Aunt Katherine; but it was hard to believe that such smartness and apparent distinction could belong to a maid.

"Miss Marshall?"

"Yes, I'm Kate Marshall. And you?"

"Bertha, Miss Elsie's maid." She turned toward a middle-aged round little Irishman in brown livery. "Timothy," she said, "it's her." Alas, for the distinction of the black toque!

Timothy stepped briskly forward and picked up Kate's suitcase, touching his cap, but giving her a quick, keenly interested glance at the same time. "Your trunk checks, if you please, Miss?" he said, holding out his free hand for them.

"Why, there isn't a trunk. The suitcase is all."

"Didn't the trunk catch this train?" Bertha asked, and added in a commiserating tone, "Service is wretched—Miss Frazier says so."

"I didn't have any trunk at all. The suitcase holds everything."

Bertha's ejaculation of surprise was suddenly turned into a flow of tactful words. "All the better, all the better. That makes things very simple, very simple. We've only to go out to the automobile then, and we'll be in Oakdale in no time."

Little round Timothy led the way with the bag and book, Kate followed him, and Bertha came behind her. She was not used to walking in processions like this, and she felt distinctly strange and lonely. But the thought that Elsie might be waiting in the car braced her up. Even so she couldn't imagine why Elsie hadn't come in and been the first to greet her at the gate. If she were Elsie she would never sit calmly waiting out in the car.

But the car was empty. It was a very handsome, big, luxurious affair, painted a light glossy brown, the very shade of Timothy's uniform. It had a long, low body, much shining nickel plate, windshields before the back seat as well as the front, and Great Aunt Katherine Frazier's monogram in silver on the door.

Timothy held back the monogrammed door while Kate stepped in. Then he slid into the driver's seat, leaving Bertha to follow him. So there was Kate bobbing around on the wide back seat that was richly though slipperily upholstered in smooth leather. Her baggage was in front with the servants. She had not even the cherished book to sustain her. She wondered, a little whimsically, that they had let her carry her purse.

Where was Elsie? Kate gave herself up to speculation as they crawled through the crowded city streets. They crawled, but it was smooth and beautiful crawling, for Timothy was an artist among chauffeurs. Kate looked all around her interestedly and happily in spite of the sharpness of her disappointment at Elsie's absence. But although it was exciting and stimulating to her to be moving through the streets of the big city she realized the heat uncomfortably and, used to her high hill air, was over-conscious of the unsavoury odours that met her on every side. She unbuttoned and threw back her cape and resisted just in time an impulse to lift her hat from her head by the crown, the way a boy does, and toss it into a corner of the seat so that her head might be a little cooler. But another inclination she did not resist in time. She leaned forward and spoke to Bertha over the windshield: "Elsie, Miss Elsie, couldn't she come? Is she well?" she asked.

What an idiotic question! Why was she always saying things so abruptly, things she hardly meant to say! Bertha turned her smooth, distinguished-looking profile. "She is very well. She will be at dinner."

Now they were out of the city and they gained speed; but they gained almost without Kate's noticing, for the car was so luxurious and Timothy was such an artist. But when she observed how the trees and fences and houses were beginning to rush by she braced her feet against the nickel footrail and laid her arm along the padded armrest. She leaned back, relaxed. She began to feel that she quite belonged in the car, as though such conveniences had always been at her service, almost as though private chauffeurs and ladies' maids were an everyday matter. Or was she dramatizing herself? Anyway, it was fun and very, very new. She hoped there would be time to write her mother all about it to-night. She profoundly wished the Hart boys could see her!

But Bertha had turned her smooth profile again. "We are just entering Oakdale," she informed her, speaking impersonally, so decorously that it might have been to the air. And instantly Kate's composure and assurance were shivered, her relaxed muscles tensed themselves, her mind became just one big question mark.

Oakdale was a charming suburb. Most of the houses seemed to have lawns and gardens that justified the name of "grounds," and wealth spoke on every side, but in a tone of good taste and often even beauty. Elms and maples lined the street down which the adventurer's chariot was bowling.

Oh, which house, which house was Great Aunt Katherine's? Would Elsie be standing in the doorway? Would Kate know the house by that? Or would she be at a window, or keeping a watch for them on some garden wall?

They suddenly swerved from the main residential street and rolled down a delightful lane bordered by older, more mellowed houses. At the very end of the lane, before a large white house with green blinds, the car came to a stop.

What a gracious, dignified house it was, and every bit as imposing and mansionlike as Kate's mother had described it. There were balconies gay with plants and hanging vines, tall windows, and an absence of anything ambiguous or superfluous. The wide front door, with its shining brass knocker and rows of potted plants at either side, was approached by a dozen or so wide, shallow stone stairs bordered by tall blue larkspur and a golden bell-shaped flower for which Kate did not know the name. The steps were almost upon the lane, but Kate knew that there were extensive "grounds" at the back, and somewhere there the little orchard house.

No Elsie stood at the top of those stone steps or came running around the house from the gardens at the sound of the stopping car. Not even Aunt Katherine made an appearance. Timothy held open the automobile door, Bertha took the suitcase and book, and Kate, with a "Thank you," to Timothy, started off on the last stage of her journey, that of the climb of the stone steps to her aunt's front door. Bertha followed close behind. Kate wondered whether she should ring the bell, or wait and let Bertha ring it for her. Or would Bertha open the door and they go in without ringing? Oh, dear! Why hadn't she asked her mother more explicitly about correct usage when there is a lady's maid at your heels? But then, perhaps Mother couldn't have helped her much, for certainly Mother had never been so attended. And then the inner Kate asserted herself. "Don't be a silly," it said. "How can it matter which of you rings the doorbell?—and certainly you're not going to go in without ringing. Bertha's hands are too full either to ring the bell or open the door. Ring."

But before her finger had time to reach the button, the door swung open before her as though by magic and Kate stepped in. A maid had opened the door and now stood half-concealed behind it with her face properly vacant. Kate, when she discovered her, gave her a nod and a faint "Thank you." Then she stood still in the hall, looking about for her aunt. She had almost given up Elsie for the present; but surely her aunt would come now from some part of the house hurrying to greet her with hospitality and show her her room.

But Bertha had no such idea. *She* did not look about as though expecting any one. "I will lead the way," she offered, "if you please. There are a good many turns." And still carrying Kate's suitcase she walked off up the narrow strip of thick gray velvety material that carpeted the polished stairs. Kate followed. It was a very complicated house, she decided, as they went through doors, down unexpected passages, up steps, and finally around a sharp turn, around two turns, up two steps, and Bertha threw open a door. There Bertha stood back for Kate to pass in ahead of her.

The bedroom that had been assigned to her was exquisitely lovely. It was a little room of beautiful proportions facing the "grounds." So much care had been spent on its decorations and furnishings that one never thought of all the money that had been spent *with* the care. Its three long windows, their sills almost on the floor, opened out on to a flowery balcony hung above the garden. The windows were wide open now because of the heat and stood back against the walls like doors. The finest of spiderweb lace was gathered against the panes, and at their sides hung opal-coloured curtains of very soft silk. The same colour, in heavier silk, was used in the spread for the narrow ivory bed, with its painted crimson ramblers at footboard and top. There was a low reading table by the bed and in the centre of it a little crystal lamp with an opal shade. Across from the bed and table stood an ivory dressing table reflecting the balcony's brilliant plants in its three hinged mirrors. An ivory-coloured chair with a low back and three legs was placed before the dressing table. On one creamy wall hung LePage's "Joan of Arc," and on the opposite wall a painting of a little girl with streaming hair leaping across a bright flower bed. Through a door with long crystal mirrors panelled into either side Kate glimpsed a white bathroom with a huge porcelain tub with shining taps and a rack hung thick with wide, creamy towels.

"What a heavenly room!" she exclaimed, enraptured. "Is it mine?"

"Yes, this is your bedroom." Bertha spoke almost deprecatingly of it. "But there is a sitting-room just across the hall. It is Miss Elsie's, but while you are here Miss Frazier says you are to share it. That is much more comfortable."

Kate went directly to a window, hoping to find the orchard house in its view. She was not disappointed. Beyond lawns and flower gardens there was the old orchard with its gnarled, twisted trees, and back among the trees the outlines of a little gray house. Kate was quite moved by this her first glimpse of her mother's home.

Bertha came up behind, and now was engaged in unbuttoning her cape for her and taking off her hat. But Kate was almost unconscious of these ministrations. She was unconscious, too, when Bertha turned to unpacking her bag.

"There won't be time for you to change to-night, Miss Frazier said," Bertha was informing her. "So we'll just wash you up a bit and brush your hair. Miss Frazier said you were to go down directly, and there's the first gong anyway."

A musical note was sounding through the house.

Reluctantly, Kate turned from the window. Bertha followed her into the bathroom, filled the bowl for her with water, and then stood at hand with soap and a towel. For one wild instant Kate wondered whether Bertha meant to wash her face for her! She had a definite feeling of relief when she put the soap and the towel down at the side of the bowl and left her alone. Quickly and efficiently Kate removed the grime of travel. When she went back into her room Bertha was standing by the dressing table, brush in hand.

Kate sat down on the three-legged chair. She thought she had never looked into clearer mirrors than the three hinged ones before her. "Please, I can brush my own hair, it's so short. I would rather." Just a few quick strokes, a poke or two, and the bobbed hair with the wing brushed across the forehead was perfectly tidy and crisp.

"I'll take you to the top of the stairs," Bertha offered. "You mayn't have noticed the way very carefully as we came along."

"No, I am not sure I could find it. But tell me first, where does that door, the other door, in the bathroom go?"

"Oh, that's Miss Elsie's door."

"Miss Elsie's room! So near! Oh, do you suppose she's in there?"

"Why, I don't know. I dressed her for dinner before starting to town for you. She's more probably downstairs. Dinner is served three minutes after that first gong."

Kate gave one more glance toward the door that now had become of so much interest to her, before following Bertha. She was glad that she and Elsie were to sleep so near each other. Why, it was a suite of rooms they had. There was something splendid about occupying a suite of rooms. And there was even a sitting-room for them across the hall. How jolly it was and how independent! But where was Elsie?

Kate thanked Bertha when she had been guided to the top of the staircase. "Am I just to go down?" she asked, a little timidly.

"Why, yes. Miss Frazier will be in the drawing-room. It's at the left. You can't miss it."

Bertha faded discreetly back as she spoke, into the shadows of the upper hall, leaving Kate suddenly to her own resources. But after an instant's hesitation, during which the inner indomitable Kate was summoned up, she passed quietly and with dignity down the gray velvet stair carpet.

CHAPTER IV
LITTLE ORCHARD HOUSE, BEWARE!

The drawing-room extended for almost half the length of the big house. It was the largest room that Kate had ever seen or imagined outside of a castle. Just at first she could not discover her aunt in it. But soon her glance found her sitting down at the farthest end near one of the French doors that stood wide open into the garden. Her head was turned away, but the shape and pose of that head and the way she sat in her chair, with a book but not reading, reminded Kate sharply and poignantly of her mother. Why hadn't Katherine warned her that they were so much alike?

She went toward her softly because of her shyness, her feet hardly making a sound on the Persian rugs, past the tables and divans and lamps. It was seven o'clock of a July evening now, and the shadows lent a lovely charm to the big room that was peculiarly charming even in broadest daylight. Kate felt as she went toward her aunt that she was walking in a dream. And it was a very nice dream, too, for that glimpse of the likeness of her aunt to her mother had reassured her completely. All her previous ideas of her aunt were swept away, and the anticipations of this visit, which for a little had been dampened, now returned with fresh life.

Miss Frazier turned as Kate came near. Hastily she put her book, still open as Kate's mother would have, on a table at her hand and rose. She kissed Kate with warmth and dignity and then held her off, the tips of her fingers on her shoulders.

"You're not one bit like your mother," she affirmed. "Not one least bit."

"Don't accuse me," Kate said, laughing. "I would have been if I could, of course. But wouldn't it have been rather confusing to have had three of us so much alike? The names are confusing enough."

If someone could have told Kate an hour—no, two minutes—ago that on first meeting her aunt she would speak so easily, so without self-consciousness, she would not have believed. She had expected to be constrained, awkward. But then she had never expected Aunt Katherine to be so agreeable as she apparently was.

Aunt Katherine was smiling quite brilliantly. Kate had instantly touched and pleased her. "Does it really seem to you that I am anything like your mother?"

Kate nodded. But even as she nodded, she saw the difference suddenly. Aunt Katherine was taller, of course; but that was not it. Her firm, squarish chin was not neutralized by melting gray eyes as Katherine's was. Aunt Katherine's eyes were dark and their expression echoed the strong chin; it was a sure expression, penetrating and above all intellectual. And the lines about the mouth and eyes were lines that Katherine would never have at any age. They were lines of loneliness and trouble.

Even as Kate was thinking all this—lightning-quick thinking it was, of course—she saw the lines deepen and the mouth and eyes harden perceptibly. "It is past dinner time. Didn't Elsie come down with you?" The hardening was not for Kate's tardiness; it was for Elsie's.

"I haven't seen her. I don't believe she was in her room or she would have heard me."

"Haven't seen Elsie? That is strange! She must be in the orchard or somewhere, and not realize the time."

Aunt Katherine moved to the garden door, her hand still on Kate's shoulder. "There she comes now, from the orchard."

They stepped over the sill and waited for Elsie on the stone flags outside. She was floating through the gardens directly from the orchard. Floating is a better word for it than hurrying because she was such a light and airy creature and above all so graceful. Her approach was almost in the nature of a dance. She was dressed in white, a narrow belt of periwinkle blue at the low waistline.

It was evident when she came nearer that she had not seen the two waiting for her. Her eyes were dropped a little and she was smiling! There was a radiance of happiness about her. At first, in this impression of her, happiness was even more obvious than prettiness. But she was pretty, too, quite enchantingly pretty. Kate, who was not pretty herself, loved it all the more in others. Her appreciation always leapt to meet it.

Elsie was slim, with a fairy grace of face and figure. Her hair, a net of sunlight even now in the growing dusk, was tied at her neck, and its curls straying on her shoulders and at her cheeks shone like fairy gold. Her face was delicately moulded and faintly tinted. It was her chin that struck Kate most. It was an elfin, whimsically pointed chin. In fact, she was such an exquisite creature that Kate, standing there waiting for the instant when she should look up and their eyes meet, felt as though her own sturdy young body belonged to another world.

But Elsie was so absorbed in her happiness that she did not raise her eyes until she was almost upon them. It was Aunt Katherine's voice that recalled her, and she stopped short a few feet from where they were standing. "Well, Elsie?"

Then at last the eyes of the destined comrades met! Kate was smiling, the corners of her mouth uptilted little wings. Her whole face spoke her delight in Elsie's extraordinary prettiness and her own expectation of comradeship. No one could have missed what her look meant. But Elsie's response was a strange one. Instantly the elfin smile vanished, the elfin chin became set, the pretty face and violet eyes hardened. But she took the few remaining steps forward and gave Kate her hand. In a correctly polite but delicately cool way she said, "How do you do?"

Aunt Katherine showed some chagrin at that tone. "This is your cousin, Elsie," she said. "You are not going to stand on any formality with a cousin who has come for the express purpose of being cousinly. Dinner was announced some minutes ago. Let us go in."

But what had happened to Kate? She hardly knew herself. She had turned sick, physically sick and faint, when Elsie had looked at her so coolly and indifferently. No one had ever treated her so in all her life before. She had had spats, of course, with her contemporaries, now and then. There had been days when either Sam or Lee or some girl in school refused to speak to her. There had been angry glances, sharp words. But she had never been treated like this. Nothing before had ever turned her *sick*.

As they moved down the long drawing-room and across the hall to the dining-room Kate asked herself desperately whether she had imagined it all. Could she have heard Elsie's voice aright? Was the cool, hard glance from Elsie's eyes insultingly indifferent? How could it be? Why should it be? What had she done? She had done just nothing at all. There was no reason in the world for Elsie to hate or despise her. And so, fortified by her reason and by the wise inner Kate that never wholly forsook her, Kate decided before they reached the dining-room that it *had* been imagination—partly, anyway. Elsie might not have liked her looks at first, but she had no reason to hate her.

Even so, she did not have the courage to look directly at Elsie when they were finally seated at the table. They were in high-backed carved Italian chairs at a narrow, long, black, much-oiled table. In the centre of the table two marvellously beautiful water lilies floated in an enormous shallow jade bowl. The napkin that Kate half unfolded in her lap was monogrammed damask and very luxurious to her fingers' touch. The dinner was simple, as simple as the dinners to which Kate was accustomed at home, but it was served with such dignity by a lacy-capped and aproned waitress that before they were finished with the prune-whip dessert Kate felt they had banqueted.

Very early in the meal Kate learned that she need not avoid looking directly at Elsie, for Elsie's own eyes were averted. Apparently she was languidly interested in the portraits on the opposite wall. At any rate, her gaze was always just a little above Kate's head or to the right or left of her shoulder. When Aunt Katherine spoke to her she looked at her as she replied. But aside from those polite and clearly spoken answers, she contributed nothing to the conversation.

In contrast to Elsie Aunt Katherine was giving her whole mind to being entertaining and making Kate feel at home. She drew her out about the life in Ashland, the barn that had so ingeniously been turned into a house, Kate's school in Middletown, the Hart boys, their mother and father, the life at Ashland College, everything that concerned Katherine and Kate. Although Kate hardly realized it, during the course of that first meal she had given her aunt a pretty complete picture of her background, and incidentally of herself.

Just as the finger bowls were brought in Aunt Katherine said, "The little orchard house beyond the garden was your Grandfather Frazier's, you know, Kate. You will want to explore it, I imagine. To-morrow at breakfast I shall give you the key."

Kate was delighted. "Oh, may I go into it? Mother wasn't at all sure it wouldn't be rented. She wanted me to see it if I possibly could, and tell her all about it."

"Of course it's not rented. It is too much part of my grounds, altogether too connected with everything here. A family there would be intolerable. And besides, I consider that the house belongs to your mother. It is only waiting for her."

But now the eyes of the two girls did meet for the second time. Kate gasped. Fear and anger spoke in Elsie's direct stare. And Kate was sure she was not imagining now—all the delicate tint had been swept from Elsie's face. She was pale.

They got up at that minute and followed Aunt Katherine from the dining-room. Elsie turned her head away as they walked. But Kate was too curious now to be definitely unhappy. She wanted only to know the reason of Elsie's behaviour. And she surprised herself more than a little by finding herself drawn to the sulky, ungracious, frightened girl. Nothing was at all the way she had dreamed it and expected it, it is true. But in some ways it was better. Elsie was more of a *person* than her dreams had made her, and friendship with her, if only they ever did become friends, might be quite wonderful. Kate did not think this out. It was just her feeling.

In the drawing-room Aunt Katherine sat down at her reading table and picked up her book. "It is after eight," she told the girls, "and I'm sure Kate should go to bed early. But you may walk in the garden together a little first."

Now Kate glimpsed the Aunt Katherine of tradition. Neither she nor Elsie had any thought but to obey the command. They went out together to walk in the garden. "Just like that," Kate said to herself, inwardly smiling. But there was no rebellion in her thought. She distinctly liked Aunt Katherine and was ready to take commands from her. And this command was particularly welcome. Now Elsie *must* unbend! Now they must find each other.

For a minute they walked in silence and then Kate said, "Let's go into the apple orchard. I want to see my mother's house nearer. Do you know I can hardly wait until morning when I shall see it inside, too. Mother has told me so much about it!"

"It isn't your mother's house," Elsie answered quite unexpectedly. "It's Aunt Katherine's. And there's nothing to see in the dark. Just a little old gray house with weeds in the front walk. Even the road to it is all grown over with grass now, for no one goes there ever."

"I want to see it all the same. It's where my mother and my grandmother and my grandfather lived. I'm going whether you come or not."

"Oh, all right," Elsie acquiesced, sulkily. "But a lot you'll see in the dark."

It was just as Elsie had said. It was a little old gray house set down in the centre of the apple orchard with no road leading to it. And weeds stood high in the gravel front walk.

"Why, it's a fairy house by starlight!" Kate exclaimed, quite forgetting Elsie's mood in her own.

Elsie spoke in a rather high voice then, a voice that carried all through the orchard: "If it is a fairy house," she called, "Fairies, beware! Orchard house, beware! If there are fairies in the house put out all lights, hurry away. Aunt Katherine's nieces are here and Aunt Katherine doesn't want the house occupied."

Kate was surprised but quickly pleased, too. Elsie had entered into a game whole-heartedly. Perhaps she was just an ordinary girl, after all! Perhaps she had been imagining absurd things about her. This Elsie calling out into the starry dimness, warning the little house of their approach, was Elsie as she should be, with her fairy-gold curls and elfin chin.

Kate involuntarily drew nearer to her. And then she raised her voice and called in her turn to the little orchard house. "But Aunt Katherine's not here," she called. "She is deep in a deep book. So light all your lights, if you wish, look out of your windows, open your doors. Little enchanted house, wake up!"

She was laughing as she finished and holding Elsie's hand, for she was quite carried away by her own fancy. This was the kind of nonsense she loved, and the little house did seem alive and awake. She *felt* it responding there in its dim starlight!

Elsie allowed her hand to be held. But she cried, softly, but still in a carrying voice, "No, no, no. Don't look out! Don't wake up. There are two of us here. Two. Not one!"

And then the girls stood silent. The game had become so real that Kate would not have been at all astonished to see fairy lights at the windows, to hear windows opening and fairy laughter. But she heard nothing except the crickets in the uncut grass and Elsie's hurried breathing.

"Come," she whispered. "Let's go all around the house"—and off she started, still holding Elsie's hand. Elsie could only go, too. And at the back of the house, the side that was in view only of the orchard and vacant fields beyond, Kate noticed two windows wide open in the second story.

"Does Aunt Katherine let those windows stay open like that?" she asked, curiously. "Those are the windows in the study. I know from Mother's telling. Suppose it should rain to-night? It must be an oversight. Let's go back and get the key from Aunt Katherine now to-night and close them for her. Won't it be fun to go in by starlight, just we two alone!"

Elsie shook her head violently and pulled her hand away at the same time. There was a break in her voice almost as though she were in danger of bursting into tears.

"You needn't go being a busybody the very first hour you are here," she exclaimed. "I guess Aunt doesn't need your advice about such things. Come away. Come out of the orchard."

Kate followed her, nonplussed, at sea. "What is the matter?" she demanded. "What are you afraid of, Elsie Frazier?" Then, stopping suddenly, "What was that? Listen!" Surely a door had closed softly up there in the room with the windows open!

"What was what?"

"Didn't you hear?"

"No, of course I didn't hear anything."

"A door closed up there."

"Nonsense! How could a door close up there?"

"Well, it did. I heard it just as plain. But perhaps it was a breeze that closed it. Only I don't feel any breeze."

"It must have been a breeze."

"Well, it was a *careful* breeze. It shut the door ever so gently. Quite as though a door knob was turned. Oh, Elsie, do you suppose it is fairies—or something weird?"

"I don't suppose anything. And Aunt Katherine will be expecting us in. Come."

As they went Kate turned to look back several times at the orchard house. But no fairy lights twinkled for her in the windows, no doors or windows opened, no fairy stood on the doorstone beckoning her back. It was just a little old gray house in an orchard. But even so Kate felt it *alive*, awake somehow. Elsie could not spoil her feeling about it.

Just outside the lighted drawing-room Elsie turned about and faced Kate. She was not quite so tall and she was slighter. But her whole body was drawn up with extraordinary force and her face, in spite of its delicate elfin quality, was determined.

"Kate Marshall," she said in a quiet tone, "you're not to say one word to Aunt Katherine about those windows. Not one single word! And what's more, you're not to use the key that she will give you to-morrow. It's not your mother's house any more. You'll only be disappointed. There's nothing of her in there at all. I shall hate you and hate you and HATE you if you use that key. You've got to promise me."

Kate did not flinch before this unexpected attack. But she was amazed. "Of course I sha'n't promise you," she contradicted. "You're a silly to think you can make me. What's the matter with you, anyway?"

Elsie still looked at her, but her firmness, her determination melted. Her lips trembled. Unshed tears glistened in her eyes. When she spoke her tone was changed completely. "Please, please," she besought Kate. "You are just a girl even if you are—well, even if you are Kate Marshall. Please promise me that you'll wait a week before exploring the orchard house. After that I won't care. Go and live in it, if you like. But just for a week, promise me."

"No, I won't promise." But Kate was softening. "I won't promise. But perhaps, since you care so much, I won't go in to-morrow or the next day. Perhaps I'll stay away a week. Only I think you'll have to tell me *why*."

But Elsie shook her head. "I can't tell you why. You'll know for yourself within a few days. You've promised?"

"I have not promised. And I think you ought to explain to me. Are you sure you won't? I'm a pretty good person at keeping a secret. If I knew, I *might* promise."

Elsie shook her head. Kate saw the tears still glistening in her eyes. She felt brutal to have made a fairy cry!

"Don't, don't cry," she begged softly. "I won't use the key to-morrow, anyway. I promise you that. And I'll tell you before I do use it. I don't see why I shouldn't put it off for a week if you care so much. I'm not a pig."

"And you won't even prowl around the orchard house during that week?"

Kate, instantly forgetting her momentary pity, grew hot. "I never prowl. What a nasty word!"

"You prowled to-night."

"I didn't. We were playing a game with the house. I'm going in."

With high-held head, flaming cheeks, and bright eyes Kate stepped into the drawing-room. Elsie was at her side, cool, calm, no trace of recent tears. In spite of Kate's flash of real anger Elsie was well satisfied with the outcome of their "walk in the garden." For she felt that Kate would be one to keep her word. Elsie might breathe freely, for a day more at any rate, and not live in hourly terror of the discovery of her secret, and the secret of the orchard house.

Aunt Katherine had been watching them through the glass of the long door. She smiled, apparently well pleased, as they came in now. She said, "I am glad that you are getting acquainted. You should have a very nice month together, you two. Kate must be tired, and I advise you both to go right to bed. Breakfast is at quarter to eight."

"She was watching us while we talked at the door," Elsie whispered as they went up the stairs. "She thought we couldn't leave off talking. She imagines we're bosom friends already."

But Kate walked on up with a set face. She did not trouble to answer.

CHAPTER V
KATE MAKES UP A FACE

As they neared their doors Elsie said, "Please tell Bertha if she's in your room that I shall be in the sitting-room when she's through helping you. I'm going right to bed then."

She stopped with her hand on the knob. "Wouldn't you like to see the sitting-room? It's yours, too, now."

Kate looked in as Elsie opened the door and stood back. Now she knew why Bertha had said that room was more "comfortable" than her bedroom. In contrast to it her bedroom was almost nun-like. There were deep chairs upholstered in gay cretonne, cretonne with parrots and poppies and birds of paradise glowing against its yellow background. There was even a little lounge, heaped with yellow pillows, drawn up under the windows. In the centre of the room stood a square cherry-wood reading table, and the walls were almost lined with bookshelves already about one third filled with books. On the table stood a glass bowl filled with red roses. A Japanese floor lamp cast a mellow light over everything. In one corner a practical old Governor Winthrop desk with many drawers and a wide writing leaf drew Kate's eyes. Imagine having a desk like that just for one's own!

But she did not show her appreciation of the room. She simply glanced about it, as Elsie seemed to expect her to, and then muttering a crusty "good-night" crossed the hall to her own room.

Bertha was waiting for her there. Evidently Aunt Katherine had instructed her that Kate would retire early. The opal lamp by the bed was shedding its delicate radiance through the room, the bed was turned down, Kate's dressing gown and nightgown were spread across its foot, and her bedroom slippers stood near at hand. Her bag had long since been unpacked and put away. The "King of the Fairies" and the mystery story—Sam and Lee's gift—lay on the bed table under the lamp.

Kate was very glad of her own cool, clear little room. She liked it better than all that colour and ease across the hall. And in any case she would never be able to share that other room with Elsie. She determined not to go into it at all—no, not even to look over the books!

"Miss Elsie is in the sitting-room," she told Bertha. "She said to tell you that when you were ready she would go to bed. I don't need any help, truly."

"Sha'n't I even brush your hair, Miss Kate? That is so restful."

"You've unpacked for me. Thank you very much. My short hair doesn't need much brushing."

So, reluctantly, for Miss Frazier had requested her to attend to both girls equally, Bertha took her dismissal. In a minute Kate heard voices on the other side of Elsie's door. Then Elsie opened the door and looked in through the bathroom.

"Aunt Katherine says we're to leave these doors open," she informed Kate, calmly. "That is so you won't be lonely."

Kate nodded an "all right." But to herself she said, "I'd be a heap less lonely if you'd close the door and I'd never see your face again."

She undressed well out of sight of Elsie's room. When she was in nightgown, dressing robe, and slippers, she sat down on the three-legged ivory stool, before the hinged mirrors, brush in hand. She was surprised by the expression of her own face as it looked back at her grimly out of the glass. All its humour, its *charm*, was gone. She was just a rather plain young girl. And as she looked at this disenchanted reflection it suddenly went misty and blurred. She saw tears rising in its eyes.

With an angry hand she dashed them away and stuck out her tongue at the blurred face in the mirror. Then came her own laugh, the eyes crinkling to slits, the mouth freed from its set lines and lifting wings in a smile.

"Idiot," she whispered. "To cry about her! She's a stuck-up little pig, but you needn't become a grouchy glum just for that. Be yourself in spite of her."

But as she went toward the windows to push them a little farther back, for the night was a warm and beautiful one, she turned her head and looked through the open doors into Elsie's room. Elsie was sitting before her own dressing table, a replica of Kate's. She was in an exquisitely soft-looking pink dressing gown edged about the neck and the long flowing sleeves with swansdown. Bertha stood behind her, brushing her curls with long, even strokes. The eyes of the two girls met in Elsie's glass. Flashingly, Kate was glad she had made up a face and got it over with; otherwise she would certainly have made up just the same face now, at Elsie, before thinking.

The pairs of eyes held each other in the glass for an instant. It must have been something deceiving in the twin lights glowing at either side of Elsie's mirror, or in the glass itself, Kate decided afterward, but for that instant it seemed that a *comrade* had looked questioningly out of the mirror at her! But the hidden comrade, if such it was, vanished even before Kate had time to turn away.

What a delicious bed Aunt Katherine had given her! She delighted in its scented linen and light covers. She punched the fluffy pillows up into a bolster, slipped out of her dressing gown and in between the smooth, lavender-scented sheets. Sitting there against the pillows she took "The King of the Fairies" on to her knee. She couldn't sleep quite yet, she knew. Why, at home she seldom went to bed before her mother, and now it was not yet nine. The very sight, even the feeling of this book in her hands filled her with a happy stir deep in the far wells of imagination. She opened it casually. Any place would do since she already knew it practically by heart. The very sight of the smooth, clearly printed pages with their wide margins freed her. She was ready for space now and clear, disentangled adventurings into light.

Although the book was titled "The King of the Fairies" it was not at all a fairy story for children. Kate had only just reached the age when it could be cared about. It began with a girl and a boy quarrelling on a fence in a meadow. It was a real quarrel, a horrid quarrel with hot and sharp and bitter words. But it is interrupted by a tramp happening by. He asks them a direction and they stop their recriminations for the time to point him his way scornfully. Accepting their directions he still tarries a while to ask them if they themselves don't want some pointing. Then the story, the marvellous story begins. He points to an elder bush and asks them what it is. They tell him glibly. Then he gets on to the fence between them and with his eyes level with theirs asks them to look again. Everything is changed for the girl and boy in that instant. They begin seeing as the tramp sees. They are in Paradise or Fairyland: the author himself makes no clear distinction. But the elder bush is now much more than an elder bush. And the meadow is full of a life the girl and boy had never suspected. There are other beings moving in it, fairy beings, perhaps. Not only is the invisible made visible to the girl and boy seeing as the tramp sees, but the, until then at least, partly visible—the brook, the trees, the very stones and the elder bush—are seen to have more *life* than could be suspected. And all colours are changed, too. The boy and girl are seeing things in a new spectrum.

Finally the three get down from the fence and wander about in this Fairyland that has always been here truly but is only now seen. The book is their day in the meadow. And when you have turned the last page you do not remember it as a *book*. You remember it as a day in Fairyland or Paradise—or as a day on which you saw things clear. And you never doubt for a minute that the author himself is one who has certainly seen like that. Perhaps he only saw it in a flash, but he did see for himself and with his own eyes.

In the end the boy and girl return to the fence and the tramp departs on the way they had pointed out to him. But as he goes, he turns about when he gets to the elder bush and they realize in that last glance from his eyes that he is the King of the Fairies. Then as he turns again and walks on, as long as he is in their sight, he is simply a common tramp.

But their quarrel has dropped for ever dead between them. A boy and a girl who have actually walked in Fairyland together and seen things clear have nothing to quarrel about, and so long as they both shall live can have nothing to quarrel about again.

And though they had surely seen things clear for a whole day in the meadow—the sun had risen to the meridian and gone down into the west while they wandered—now when they look at each other there is no indication that a minute has passed. The sun is where it was at the height of their quarrel! And so it appears that the tramp's arrival and stay and departure and their whole day in the meadow was squeezed into perhaps one straight meeting of their eyes as they quarrelled.

But they do not spend themselves in wonder. This boy and girl are Wisdom's own children, in spite of the momentary silliness that had plunged them head-first into the darkness of an enmity; they accept the gods' gifts. And for a boy and a girl who have spent a day in Fairyland together, or for that matter only spent a minute there together, the gods' gift is marriage.

Katherine, when she had finished the book, had said that it was the most perfect love story she had ever read; she wished she were rich enough to give it to all the lovers she knew. And she said, too, that the author must be a very wonderful person, a great man in some field of life. Perhaps that was why he had not signed his name to the work.

As Kate read now, the conversation between Elsie and Bertha in the next room was a humming undertone to her thoughts. She could not have caught their words if she had listened. But she had no inclination to listen. She was moving in a world where quarrels and bitter feelings were an impossibility. She was seeing things through the eyes of the King of the Fairies. She was in the meadows that she knew at home, feeling the larger life there that the King of the Fairies had made known to her. She was standing, tall, in the body of an elm tree, spreading with its leaves to the sun, feeling with its roots into the vibrating ground.

Suddenly a voice came to her. It was a long way she rushed back to find the voice. Bertha was standing beside her bed.

"Shall I turn out your light, Miss Kate? Or do you wish to read?"

Kate did not know that Bertha had come into the room at all. Elsie's light was out, and if the doors through must be left open, Kate's light would disturb her. Of course she must put out her light and try to sleep. She was on the verge of saying, "I will put out my own light, thanks," but the meadow from which she had rushed back had, oddly enough as some might think, put her into more perfect harmony with her own restricted four walls. So she said, "You may put the light out, thank you." And she did not even smile to herself when Bertha bent over the table and pulled at the little chain that was much nearer Kate's reach than hers. She accepted the service naturally, since such acceptance was Aunt Katherine's wish and the purpose of Bertha's presence here.

"Good-night," Bertha spoke out of the sudden darkness.

"Good-night," Kate answered. Then soft footfalls, and she was alone in the room.

But though "The King of the Fairies" had done a good deal for Kate it had not had time to do enough to make her call a "good-night" to Elsie. Suppose Aunt Katherine knew the two girls were going to sleep without a word to each other!

From her bed, now that the room was dark, Kate could see the dim apple orchard under starlight. She rose on her elbow and strained her eyes for the outlines of the little orchard house. She found it by hard looking. How mysterious, how lonely, still how alive out there it stood. And she *had* heard a door close softly, just as though a door knob had turned as they stood below those open back windows. And why were those windows open? Elsie knew, Kate was sure. The little orchard house harboured some secret of Elsie's.

But what was that! Kate sat up in bed and bent toward the window, her eyes straining. A light, flickering, was moving down through the house! Kate watched it as it went by several windows, breathless. Soon it disappeared altogether, and a second after Kate thought she heard the front door of the little orchard house softly closing, or opening; but that must have been fancy, for the orchard house was much too far away for a sound of that quality to carry to her.

As she curled down into bed again her eyes crinkled with her smile in the darkness. Well, here was mystery. She would write Sam and Lee that she would save their mystery story for duller times. Now she was living in one!

CHAPTER VI
"I WILL PAY FOR IT"

Kate was waked next morning by Elsie moving about in her room. She opened her eyes quickly and sat up. To her surprise Elsie was dressed and ready for the day. She looked as fresh as the July morning in a blue and white gingham, white sport shoes and stockings. Her hair was pinned up at her ears, and that made her look older but not less pretty than last night.

Kate was not a girl to wake up with a grudge on a morning like this, or on any morning, in fact. So she sang out now, "Hello!"

But Elsie, apparently, had not been mellowed by sleep. She responded to the "hello" with a nod. Then, much to Kate's surprise, she came directly to the bed and picked up "The King of the Fairies" from the table there.

"Bertha told me you had borrowed my book," she said. "I don't mind your borrowing books. But I think you ought to ask. And Aunt Katherine didn't give me this one. I'm going to read outdoors before breakfast, and I want 'The King of the Fairies,' if you don't mind."

Kate laughed. "It's my copy, not yours," she said. "Mother and I gave it to each other last Easter. It's a perfectly great book, Mother thinks, and I brought it with me here because I love it so."

Elsie was standing directly in the gilded morning sunlight. Kate had just waked up and her eyes were still a little dazed from sleep. That may account for her seeing again, flashingly, the comrade she had surprised in the mirror last night. Surely Elsie's whole being in that flash radiated comradeship. And there was something more. Kate could not remember, but sometime in her life—it felt a long time ago—she had exchanged glances with that golden comrade! Or had it been just a vivid dream she had had, or perhaps only the ideal she had set up in her mind of the perfect comrade?

But Elsie almost instantly moved out of the sunlight nearer the bed, and everything was as before.

"Please pardon me," she said coldly. "I don't know why it never entered my head that you might have a copy of your own. That was stupid of me. I'll see you at breakfast."

"So it is still on," Kate told herself, as Elsie left the room. "She hates me. She hates me just awfully. And that was awfully rude about the book, even if it had been hers! How *could* she be so rude—to a *guest*? She is afraid of me, too. She is afraid I will discover the secret of the orchard house. Why, perhaps she doesn't hate me, personally at all. Mayn't it be just fear that makes her like that? For she has no reason to hate me, and of course if she has some secret in the orchard house she has every reason to think I may discover it. For I do mean to explore it thoroughly when I get around to it."

Somehow the conviction she had come to, that fear rather than personal dislike was ruling Elsie's conduct, comforted her. Moreover, it was a perfect morning—sunshine, a light breeze at the curtains, birds carolling (how had she ever slept through the noise those birds were making?) and the room pervaded by flower scents from balcony and gardens. It was with a light heart, then, that Kate allowed Bertha to run her bath, lay out her clothes, and finally even brush the bobbed hair. Such unneeded service seemed absurd to Kate, but it was in the order of this household, and some fresh sweetness she had brought from sleep made her eager to harmonize herself as much as possible with the world she had come back to. But even so, in a minute when Bertha's back was turned, Kate grabbed the brush from the dressing table and gave a quick, surreptitious stroke that turned the bang Bertha had created into a wing across her brows; for Bertha, experienced lady's maid as she was, had not caught the knack of *that* so quickly.

It was with a heart as bright as the morning that Kate finally went down the long stairs just as the soft-toned gong was sounding. There was no sign of breakfast being laid in the dining-room, so she wandered about the house, in and out of the rooms she had only glimpsed through open doors last night.

Everything was quite beautiful. Kate knew that Aunt Katherine had once been determined to "go in for art seriously." But at that time money had been lacking for such a design, and she had with keen disappointment submitted to fate and become a school teacher. When wealth had suddenly come to her everyone thought she would, of course, take up study with some great master and become an artist. But this never came about. Perhaps the first disappointment had been too keen; perhaps in giving up her hope so definitely she had made it impossible for herself ever to renew it under any conditions. But now, wandering about these rooms that Aunt Katherine had made, Kate realized that she had turned artist in a way. Instead of painting on canvas she had created beauty in her environment. For her home was like a warmly painted picture with beautiful lights and shadows. And Kate soon felt as though she were walking around in a picture. The morning sunshine outside was its great gilded frame. That was how the utter silence and absence of human beings in these big downstairs rooms explained itself to her fancy; somehow she had walked into a picture painted by her great aunt, a picture hung up somewhere in an enormous gilded frame. This fancy stirred her imagination and she pretended so hard to herself that it became quite real.

That is why she almost started when she finally did hear voices and the clink of china. Coming out of the picture into everyday life, suddenly like that, was something of a jar. And she was probably late for breakfast wherever it was being served. She hurried her steps and found Aunt Katherine and Elsie already at the meal. They were sitting at a little table under a peach tree growing up between the flags of a terrace just outside a sunny breakfast-room. How delightful! Kate was glad now to step down out of the picture.

Aunt Katherine greeted her with a welcoming smile. And having just stepped down out of Aunt Katherine's picture Kate felt that she understood her, that they were very close to each other really. How different, and how pleasantly different, Great Aunt Katherine was proving herself from Kate's preconceived ideas of her.

Kate took the little garden chair waiting for her and unfolded her napkin. Coffee was percolating visibly in two large glass globes set one on top of the other before Aunt Katherine. The silver sugar bowl and cream pitcher turned all the sunlight that found them into a million diamond sparkles. A half grapefruit with ice snuggled about it was at Kate's place. Kate lifted the slender pointed spoon made just for grapefruit, and gratefully tasted the tart pulp and juice.

"Elsie might have shown you the way," Aunt Katherine was saying. "I thought of course you would come down together."

"I am sorry I was late. But it was fun wandering around in the house trying to find you." And then Kate told them all about how she had felt herself in a picture.

Aunt Katherine was pleased. "Was it really like that to you, my house?" she asked.

"Oh, yes! and more so than I know how to say. Most of the windows and doors open, the glimpses of tree branches and flowers and sky, the light and shade in the rooms, all the flowers in vases in surprising places, the colours of everything, the hangings——"

Kate stopped, embarrassed by her own enthusiasm, or perhaps discomfited by Elsie's cool gaze. But she had said more than enough to give Aunt Katherine very real and deep pleasure.

"Then I see," she told Kate, "why you did not mind wandering about alone or our seeming inhospitality. And I think your dress, my dear, fitted into the picture. It is a very poetic dress."

Kate flushed with pleasure. "Mother would love to hear you say that," she said. "We made it out of the new chintz curtains in her bedroom. You see I had to have some dresses, and there were the curtains. Mother thought——"

But at mention of her mother Kate saw in morning light what she had failed to see last night in lamplight: the deepening of pain lines around Aunt Katherine's eyes and mouth, a cloud of pain somehow in her face. So she broke off her account of Katherine's ingenuity.

"I'm glad you like it," she finished lamely.

"I have brought you the key to the orchard house," Aunt Katherine said, as though it were a matter she would like to be done with quickly. "Elsie will show you all over it and around it. Then I have an errand at the post office I wish you girls would do for me. I have a very busy morning ahead. The car is at your disposal this morning, and I should think you would take a good long ride. It is really too warm to do anything more energetic. At least, it promises to be a very warm day."

Kate looked at the key which Aunt Katherine had handed her. It was an old-fashioned brass key, clumsy and heavy but not too big to go into her pocket. When she had tucked it away there she raised defiant eyes to Elsie. But her defiance suddenly turned to pity. Elsie looked so troubled!

Aunt Katherine with a word of apology to the girls picked up the mail now lying at her place and began reading the one or two personal letters she found among the circulars, pleas for charity, and advertisements. Kate leaned toward Elsie and said quickly and softly, "Don't worry. You're safe to-day and to-morrow, too, and for as long as you mind, I guess. If I see the little house sometime, what does it matter when?"

Elsie nodded to signify that she had caught the very low words, and her face cleared.

"Ungrateful thing! She might at least have thanked me," Kate reflected.

But very soon she learned that Elsie was thanking her for that impulsive gesture of generosity in her own way. When they joined each other in the big car that was waiting for them at the door, half an hour later, Elsie was plainly trying to force herself to be friendly and natural. But since this friendliness was forced, Kate's response to it was of necessity forced, too. Oh, how different everything was turning out between these two girls from the way Kate had dreamed it!

"Don't you think Oakdale is pretty?" Elsie asked. "People care so much about their gardens. And then the streets are all so wide and shady, and where they aren't wide they are just little lanes like ours that end perhaps in a gate or an open meadow. Those endings of streets seem romantic to me always."

"Yes, I think they are romantic," Kate agreed. "And when your lane turned all the away around and ended in the orchard, that must have been awfully romantic. I wonder why Aunt Katherine ever let the grass grow over it so that it got lost, the end of the lane!"

Something in Elsie's restrained silence at this remark made Kate realize that she had blundered. Oh, dear! She hadn't meant to. Truly! She tried to explain.

"You see it was my mother's house, Elsie. You can't know what fun it is to imagine your mother a little girl, to see for the first time the house where she was born and the places where she played. Everything about your mother's childhood—well, there's a kind of mystery about it."

Elsie deliberately turned away her face. "Oh, I'm sorry. What an idiot I am! I had forgotten about your mother! How could I be such a—brute!"

Elsie looked at Timothy's back steadily. "Don't be so sorry as all that," she replied coolly and without any apparent emotion in her voice. "My mother was killed in an automobile accident in France two years ago. But I never knew her, anyway. When I was at home she was usually somewhere else, at house-parties or sanitariums, or abroad. And I was only home for holidays. She sent me off to boarding school when I was eight. Her being dead hasn't made much difference to me. I was terribly sorry for her when they told me, that was all. She was so pretty, and too young-seeming to be a mother. And she would have hated dying! Sometimes I *ache* for her when I think of that. But that's all."

"Oh, how can you! How can you speak about a dead mother like that!" Kate's heart was crying. But she only said, after a second: "There are lots of jolly-looking girls and boys in this town. Do you know them all? They keep looking at us, but you never speak. Don't you *see* people? Mother's like that. She's so absent minded."

But even this was an unfortunate subject. Unlucky Kate!

"I know who most of them are but of course I don't know them socially."

This was amazing. "Why not?"

But here all Elsie's attempt at friendliness broke down. She turned on Kate a tigerish face. "Yes, why not?" she almost hissed. "You know very well, Kate Marshall, why not. Here's the post office."

Kate was shocked. "Well, I certainly *don't* know 'why not'," she contradicted. "I haven't the least idea—unless you treat them in the rude, horrid way you treat me."

The car had drawn up to the curb and come to a stand-still before the pride of Oakdale's civic life, its white marble post office built on the lines of a Greek temple. Elsie's only answer to Kate's denial was a shrug.

"Have you letters? And are there any errands?"

Timothy stood on the sidewalk asking for orders.

Elsie stood up quickly. "I'll post the letters myself," she answered him. Kate noticed for the first time a package that Elsie was carrying. Across the top the word "Manuscript" was written in a round hand, and the address was that of a publishing house and caught Kate's attention because it was the same publishing house that had brought out "The King of the Fairies." Kate read the large round black handwriting quite mechanically and without any motive of curiosity as Elsie stepped past her out of the car.

When Elsie was halfway up the post-office steps she turned and ran back to the curb. "Tell me," she said, "didn't Aunt Katherine ask us to do something for her? I've quite forgotten what it was."

"Yes. A dollar book of stamps and ten special deliveries. She gave you the money."

"Oh, thanks. Good for your memory."

"What is she sending to those publishers?" Kate found herself wondering when the spinning glass doors had closed on her "cousin." "There was a special delivery stamp on it, too. And it filled her mind so full that she quite forgot Aunt's errands. Can Elsie be trying to *write*? Oh, wouldn't that be exciting!"

"Now Holt and Holt's," Elsie ordered Timothy when she returned to the car.

"Holt and Holt's is a grocery store. I noticed it as we came by," Kate said. "I didn't hear Aunt Katherine say anything about groceries."

"Of course not. Julia, the cook, attends to all that over the telephone. This is my errand. Do you mind?"

Kate refused to rise to the sarcasm in Elsie's "Do you mind?"

But at the grocers' she said, "I think I'll come, too, and stretch my legs."

"All right." But Kate distinctly felt that Elsie did not at all like the idea of having her companionship in the store. However, her pride would not let her turn back now, of course.

Elsie's order was given briskly: "A head of crisp Iceland lettuce," she said, "a small bottle of salad oil, genuine Italian, half a pound of almonds, half a dozen eggs, and the smallest loaf of bread you have. Oh, yes, and a pound of flour, if you sell so little."

"Thanks," said the young clerk who had written the order down in his book.

But Elsie waited. He looked at her inquiringly. "Anything more?"

"No. But I want what I ordered."

"I thought we'd send it, of course. It will be quite a load."

"No. Please do the things up and put them into my car for me. How much is it all?"

"Oh, that's all right. You're Miss Frazier, aren't you? You folks have a charge account here."

"However, I want to pay for these things myself. Do not by any means put them on Miss Frazier's account." Elsie spoke primly but with flushed cheeks that contradicted her outward composure.

"Thought I'd just tell you. Yesterday when you came in and paid for things Mr. Holt said there must be some mistake."

"There is no mistake. And will you please put the box of eggs in a bag? Not just tie them with a string like that!"

"We're going up your way, miss, in about ten minutes. Why don't we take 'em?"

But Elsie shook her head, biting her lips with annoyance at the young man's persistence. She commanded him to put the things into the car.

"To the Bookshop now," she ordered Timothy as they started again.

At the Bookshop Kate did not speak of getting out, though it certainly attracted her more than the grocery store. But Elsie herself turned at the door. "Don't you want to come, too, Kate?" she called. "It's an awfully cunning little place."

Kate and her mother were always drawn by bookshops wherever they found them, and they spent in them during the course of a year a sum that it would have taken no budget expert to see was all out of proportion to their income. But then, Katherine always said when the subject of "budgeting" came up that it was as foolish to make rules about the spending of money as it would be to make rules about the spending of time. It was a matter for the individual, strictly. Kate followed Elsie eagerly, now.

It was such a little shop that Kate, although she immediately gravitated toward a table of books that interested her particularly, could not avoid hearing Elsie's conversation with the Bookshop woman.

"Have you Havelock Ellis's 'Dance of Life'?" she asked.

"Yes, a new order has just come in. I knew Miss Frazier wanted it and I was sending it up first thing this afternoon. Would you like to take it?"

"Yes, I'll take one for my aunt, if she ordered it. I'll take two. One is for myself, and I will pay for it."

"Your aunt always charges. Sha'n't I charge them both?"

"No, I will pay for it. How much is it?"

"Four dollars."

"Four dollars! Oh, dear! So much?"

The woman was very obliging. "Why not charge it?" she suggested again, for Elsie was looking woefully into her purse.

"No. Let me think a minute. Well, I won't buy it to-day."

Elsie's face had so fallen, she was so obviously disappointed, that Kate went over to her. "I have money," she offered. "Five dollars. You can borrow from me."

But as she spoke her glance quite unconsciously fell upon the purse opened in Elsie's hand. A little roll of crisp bills lay there for any one to see, amounting surely to more than four dollars.

"No, thanks." Elsie replied, snapping the purse shut. "Let's go home."

Kate turned it over quickly as they went back to the car. Why had Elsie acted, as she certainly had acted, as though she did not have four dollars in her purse when it was perfectly plain that she had more? And why did she want the book, anyway? Katherine had bought that book less than a week ago, and Kate had had an opportunity to look into it to find what of interest there might be for herself. She had found nothing. It was decidedly a book for adults, a rather deep book, and, to Kate's mind, a dull book. But perhaps Elsie only wanted it to give away. Anyway, she would ask no questions. It was none of her business.

Timothy showed distinct surprise at Elsie's nonchalant "Home, Timothy." And Kate understood his surprise. Aunt Katherine had given them the car for the morning and Timothy was all prepared to start off on a long drive. But Elsie had apparently forgotten about this in her worry over the book. And Kate had no impulse to remind her. If things were only as one might expect them to be, not all so strangely mysterious and unpleasant, a car at her disposal and a comrade on a beautiful summer morning like this would have seemed the height of pleasure. But such a ride with Elsie would certainly be no fun, and she did not think until it was too late that she alone with Timothy might start off on an exploring adventure.

When they got out of the car in front of their own door, Timothy, as a matter of course, expected to take the packages from the grocery store around to the servants' entrance. But Elsie held out her hands for them. He relinquished them to her, plainly puzzled. Surely they were groceries!

When the two girls stood together in the big front hall Kate said briefly: "Good-bye. I'm going out into the garden."

"Wait on the terrace outside the drawing-room and I'll come with you," Elsie responded, very unexpectedly. "First I'll just run up to my room with these bundles. I know a lot about the kinds of flowers and things in the garden. Let me show it all to you."

Kate was almost dazed by this suggestion. She had certainly been made to feel that Elsie was only too eager to get rid of her company. She stood where she had been left, wondering.

Why had Elsie taken lettuce and oil and bread and eggs and flour and nuts up to her room? What could she ever do with them up there?

"I'll not ask her about it," she promised herself, "just not a thing. But I shall write to Mother and the boys this morning. I won't tell Mother how horrid Elsie is being, though. She would be too disappointed for me. And I'm really not having such a bad time as it might sound. But I'll tell the boys just everything. They will be as mystified as I am. And to think I was dissatisfied with them for chums and wanted a *girl!* I'll appreciate them when I get back, that's certain. Oh, of course! Why didn't I think at first! Elsie doesn't trust me in the garden alone! That's why she wants to come with me. She is afraid I won't keep my promise. She's afraid I will go 'prowling' around the orchard house. I just wish I hadn't promised not to use the key. It would be something to do with this morning she's spoiled. And something to write Mother about. And it might explain some of the mystery. There *was* a light last night. I saw it plain enough. The boys will be interested in all that. How soon can I expect letters from home, I wonder?"

With these thoughts Kate went out through the cool, shady drawing-room and on to the terrace. There in the shade of some trellised wisteria she sat down on a garden bench to wait for Elsie.

CHAPTER VII
"EVEN SO——"

Elsie was a very long time in coming. As the minutes dragged themselves along Kate's cheeks began to get hot even before she realized that she was angry. But after she had waited so long that she was convinced Elsie was not coming at all she got up with a shrug. Any one who knew Kate would have seen at once that she was in no ordinary mood; for shrugs or any such Latin methods of self-expression were quite foreign to this girl, New England bred.

She went up to her room for paper. Now was the time to write to her mother and Sam and Lee. Certainly she had enough to tell them!

The door to the sitting-room across the hall was standing open and a glance assured Kate that it was empty. And while she did not actually look into Elsie's room she heard no sound and felt that Elsie was not there. But she had no idea where Bertha had put the writing paper when she unpacked the suitcase and the envelopes and stamps. She searched through the drawers of the dressing table. But there were only her ribbons, her handkerchiefs, her underclothes arranged artistically. No sign of paper or fountain pen. So, although she had meant never to go into the sitting-room, she was forced to now. Her writing materials must be in the desk there.

She found them at once. And now being in the room, she took the occasion to look all about. It was the jolliest place imaginable for a girl to call her own! And since the morning had grown rather oppressively hot it was a refuge, too; for there was a breeze on this side of the house and it was the coolest spot Kate had found herself in that morning. Tree shadows stood on the walls, and leaf shadows shook in a green, cool light. It would be very nice to sit here and write. But Kate could not bring herself to do it. She reminded herself that this was Elsie's desk and room, and therefore hateful.

Picking up her own property she hurried out and down the stairs. Once in the garden she made directly for the apple orchard. She would allow herself to walk along the edge viewing the orchard house from that angle. If Elsie called that prowling, let her! As she walked she felt the brass key in her pocket. But though now her whole mind was on the house and her desire to go into it, it never entered her head to break her promise. Elsie certainly deserved her anger, but revengeful thinking was quite outside of Kate's mentality.

When she had walked the whole length of the orchard she came to a low, broad hedge that marked the termination of Aunt Katherine's grounds. Near it she sat down, not in the orchard but in its shade, and placing her block of paper on her knee began to write.

"Dearest Mother":—And then so suddenly that it startled her, tears blotted the two words. At the same minute she heard running feet. Kate winked fast and furiously and looked up. Elsie was standing over her. She was flushed from running in the heat and her eyes were very bright and soft. Again she was radiating happiness as on Kate's first glimpse of her. On her arm swung a straw basket and one hand held a pair of shining shears. Kate felt that she would rather die on the spot than let Elsie guess that she was crying. But if Elsie saw the tears she showed no sign.

"I'm sorry I didn't get here sooner, and that I asked you to wait." She spoke in a conciliatory tone. "Truly I'm not so rude as I seemed. But I had an unexpected opportunity to attend to something that needed attention and there wasn't time to run down and tell you. It had to be done quickly. But now I'm ready. I thought as we walked around I'd cut some flowers for our rooms. Aunt Katherine likes me to keep my vases filled."

Now it was Kate who was cold and distant. Her shame in her tears made that necessary. "I'm writing to my mother," she answered. "And I don't need to be entertained a bit. Some other time I'll help you with the flowers."

Elsie's glow flickered and went out. "Very well," she said, and turned away sharply to cut some nasturtiums growing around the foot of an apple tree.

But just as she turned there came a shout from over the hedge. A boy older than themselves, in fact a young man of seventeen probably, had come to the tennis court, only a few paces beyond the hedge, with a racket and balls in his hand. He was calling to a girl on the steps of the piazza of the house next door. "Hurry up," he shouted. "Come on."

"Yes. Just a minute." The girl was bending over on the steps, tying her shoe perhaps. In a minute she had come bounding down the long slope of the lawn and joined her brother.

Kate looked at them interestedly. "Who are they?" she asked of Elsie. Elsie gave her the information without turning. "That's Rose Denton and her brother Jack. And they'd ask you to play, probably, if they saw you, and I weren't here. They just barely speak to me."

"Barely speak to you? And they live right next door?"

"Yes, queer, isn't it!" The voice above the nasturtiums was sarcastic. "Only get yourself noticed and you'll soon know them. Hope you have a good time."

Elsie straightened up, adjusted her basket on her arm, and moved away. But Kate called after her, her voice shaking with anger, "I don't know why you are so queer, Elsie Frazier, or why you haven't friends. But while I'm visiting you it isn't likely I'd play with people who won't play with you, no matter how much they asked me. That's that."

Elsie turned and walked backward now. "Well, Kate Marshall, I'm afraid you'll have just a horrid month then," she prophesied. And with a strange, almost strangled little laugh she whirled about and was really off with her basket and shears.

Kate watched her as she went, floating toward the gardens across the smooth lawn. "She walks like a dryad," she thought, "and she looks like a Dorothy Lathrop fairy." Then she smiled a little woefully at her own fancy. "She may look like a fairy but she's a horrid, stuck-up thing just the same," she reminded herself.

But she found relief for her overcharged emotions when she came to the compositions of her letter to the Hart boys. There she described Elsie just as she was and had behaved. Not one unpleasant thing that Elsie had done was forgotten. Perhaps it was rather horrid of Kate to complain so unrestrainedly and set down so much criticism. But she did not give that a thought—not then. When the letter was finished and in its envelope she pulled it out again to add a postscript.

P. S. It's all true what I have told you about Elsie Frazier, every bit. But *even so*, I don't hate her and now that I've written about her I'm not even angry any more. She's hardly said a friendly word or acted a bit as you would expect her to to a guest, but even so if she only were nice to me I'd be quite crazy about her. That isn't just because she's so pretty, either. I don't know why I feel that way, but I do. She's exactly the sort of chum I've always imagined having some day. And there's one thing good I can tell you about her. She likes "The King of the Fairies," I think. Anyway, she owns it. So what do you make of it all? And what about the light in the orchard house? And why do you suppose Elsie is so set against my using the key? And why did she buy those groceries and take them up to her room? Don't tell Mother a word I've told you about how mean Elsie is. *She* must think I'm having a *lovely* time— at least, until I know whether I can stick it out or not. K.M.

CHAPTER VIII
KATE MEETS A DETECTIVE

When Kate came to luncheon that day she was surprised to see a letter lying at her place. So soon? Why, she had not been here a day yet!

"It's not your mother's handwriting," Aunt Katherine said, a little curiously.

"No, it's from the boys. Oh, I'm so glad!"

"The boys?"

"Yes, I told you about them last night, you know. The twins. The Harts. How jolly of them to write me so soon!"

"But what can they have to tell you since yesterday?"

"It will be all about Mother, and much better than a letter from her herself because she doesn't know how to tell about herself, you know. She's always so silent on that subject. Do you mind, Aunt, if I just open it and peek?"

"Of course, my dear, read it. Elsie and I will excuse you."

But there was almost no letter inside. There was one paragraph in the exact centre of a big square sheet of yellow notepaper, written in a script so small and round and legible that it was almost print like. But the very wide margins were bordered with a series of pen sketches that told a story in its progressive action something in the way a moving picture does. It was the story of a picnic the Harts had arranged for yesterday afternoon with Katherine the guest of honour. Professor Hart, in an endeavour to rescue the lunch basket which had fallen into a brook, had evidently fallen in after it. That perhaps was the high mark in the artist's work. But the picnic had been chock full of adventure one could see at a glance; and Lee's quick humour and real art had turned even the worst mishaps into fun.

The paragraph was in Sam's hand, and began: "Dear Kate, if you are well it is well. We also are well." Apparently he had nothing whatsoever to say, but he said it cheerfully.

Kate crinkled up her eyes and laughed so wholeheartedly over the nonsense that she felt herself rude. She passed the paper to Aunt Katherine. "You will see that I can't help it," she explained.

And Aunt Katherine, after she had studied the pictures a few seconds and skimmed the paragraph, laughed, too, a light, genuinely amused laugh. "It's not only funny, though," she insisted, "it's artistic. Which boy drew these pictures?"

"Lee. He's always sketching. He means to be a real artist."

"I think he is that already. All he needs now is study. I would say he has a future if he has the will to stick to it."

Aunt Katherine now handed the letter to Elsie and turned back to Kate to remark: "Your mother, on accepting my invitation for you, mentioned the fact that you were lonely, in need of friends as much as Elsie. But I don't see how any one could be more companionable or amusing than these boys, from your descriptions and this letter."

Kate glowed at Aunt Katherine's appreciation of Sam and Lee. "Oh, Mother meant *girl* friends. There just doesn't happen to be any one near my age in Ashland. And while boys are all right, they aren't exactly the same."

Elsie had lost some of her indifference and coldness over the letter. She was almost smiling, in fact. Now she was actually smiling. Kate beamed. This was certainly the most natural minute and the happiest since her arrival. She blessed the Hart boys for having created it.

But Aunt Katherine was surprised when it developed that the girls had not been exploring the countryside in the car that morning.

"Didn't you use Timothy at all?" she asked.

"Just for errands in the town. Kate wrote letters and I picked and arranged flowers, and read 'The King of the Fairies.'"

"One would think, Elsie, you possessed only one book. When are you going to finish with 'The King of the Fairies'?"

"Oh, I don't know." Elsie's tone had fallen suddenly into sulkiness.

But though Aunt Katherine did not seem to notice the sudden chilling of the atmosphere, Kate did and spoke quickly, a trifle nervously.

"Haven't you read 'The King of the Fairies,' Aunt Katherine?"

"Why, no. It's a fairy story, a child's book. It surprises me that Elsie, a big girl of fifteen, finds it so fascinating."

"Mother finds it fascinating, too," Kate hurried to assure her. "And I know it just about by heart. Mother keeps saying it's the most beautiful love story she ever read. And even the boys like it. They felt just the way you do about its title. But once they got into it they couldn't stop. If you read it yourself you'd see why."

Kate was fairly radiant with her enthusiasm about this book. Her aunt smiled into her eager eyes. "I shall certainly look it over, then," she promised. "It must be an unusual book to inspire such loyalty."

"I'll bring my copy down and put it on your reading table right after luncheon."

"You have a copy with you! It *must* be a favourite! Thank you, Kate."

But Elsie did not offer a word to this topic. She sat, colder than ever, looking at the wall to the right of Kate's shoulder.

"As Timothy hasn't been working this morning, I think I shall have him take me in to Boston this afternoon," Aunt Katherine said, as she helped the girls to lemon ice which had just been set before her in a frosted bowl. "Driving is about the coolest thing one can do to-day. Will either or both of you come with me?"

"Oh, yes. *I* should love to." Kate was secretly relieved that with this promise she would not be thrown alone with Elsie again that afternoon. And she was even more relieved when Elsie said, "I don't believe I'll go, thank you, Aunt Katherine. I shall read or do something here."

As Kate was on her way up to get her hat for the drive she was stopped at the stair-turning by a woman who had come through a door connecting with a different staircase. She was a middle-aged, plump person with graying curly hair, in a starched black and white print dress, almost entirely concealed by a crisp white apron. It was the cook, Julia.

"How do you do, Miss Kate," she said, hurriedly, and almost in a whisper. "Excuse me, but I just had to ask how is your blessed mother? Miss Frazier never tells us anything at all. She ain't sick or anything, is she, and that's why you're here?"

Kate reassured her. "But did you know Mother?" she asked.

"Of course. We all did, 'cept Isadora. She's new since. Your mother was for ever in and out of the house and we all loved her. Didn't she ever tell you the time she broke her arm falling on the kitchen stairs? And she never cried, if you'll believe me. Only moaned just a bit, even when the doctor come and fixed it. Miss Frazier was away and old Mr. Frazier, too. So I had to manage. Didn't she ever tell you?"

Kate had to admit that she had never heard the story.

"Well, she wan't one to talk about herself, she wan't. Always interested in *you* and sort of forgot herself like."

Kate nodded at that. Evidently Julia did know her mother.

"And you say she's perfectly well? We'll all be grateful for that."

Aunt Katherine's voice came up to them from the hall at this point. She was talking to Elsie. As quickly as she had appeared, Julia whisked about and was out of the door through which she had come. But quick as a wink, and almost as if by magic, before she vanished she had produced from somewhere a gingerbread man and pushed it into Kate's hand.

Kate looked at the gift, amused, when Julia was gone. "She couldn't have realized how old I am," she thought, smiling. "She thinks I'm just Mother's 'child.'" Up in her room she hid it under her pillow.

*　　*　　*　　*　　*　　*　　*　　*

It was pleasant speeding along with her aunt toward Boston, creating their own breeze as they went through the hot July afternoon.

"Now tell me, Kate," Aunt Katherine questioned her abruptly as soon as they were on their way. "Are you and Elsie getting on well? Are you becoming friends?"

This was difficult for Kate. She hesitated. "I don't think Elsie likes me," she said finally. "She tries to be—polite, I think."

"Not like you? Nonsense! How could she help liking you?"

Kate laughed. "I suppose you *can't* like everybody," she said modestly. "But Elsie doesn't seem to like very many people. That boy and girl next door— she doesn't play with them."

"Oh, Rose and Jack Denton. You know the reason for the coldness there, of course. But you are quite different."

"No, I don't know the reason. Why hasn't she friends here? I don't know anything. She hasn't explained at all."

Aunt Katherine showed real surprise. "Do you mean your mother hasn't told you why things are difficult for Elsie? Is she as ashamed as that? Well, she feels even more strongly than I had suspected then."

Bitterness and sorrow had settled on Aunt Katherine's features.

"I don't think Mother knew anything to tell me," Kate protested. "Why are things difficult for Elsie?"

"If your mother hasn't told you, she wouldn't want *me* to. That is certain. But I am surprised she let you come, feeling so. However, since she did let you come, and you have no prejudice, Elsie has no business to include you in her rages. You are the one person in the world she should be friendly with and grateful to. And, you know, I am sure she exaggerates other people's attitude, anyway. The young people would be friendly enough if she would only go halfway."

Aunt Katherine put her hand on Kate's arm and continued earnestly: "That is one reason why I wanted you to come so much, to help us break the ice. Friday I am giving a party in your honour, Kate, an informal little dance."

Kate clasped her hands. For a minute she forgot all the mystery that had gone before in her aunt's speech.

"A dance! Oh, Aunt Katherine, how beautiful of you!" To herself she added, "Glory, glory! Already things are beginning to happen just as Mother said they would."

"I have asked fifteen boys and thirteen girls. *They have all, every one, accepted!* If that doesn't prove how mistaken Elsie is, I am a very foolish woman."

"Elsie hasn't mentioned the party to me," Kate wondered aloud.

"No. I haven't told her anything about it yet. I wanted you here and established first. I hoped that once you and she were having a happy, gay time together, she would soften, feel more in the mood. Most of the young people I have asked she had met when visiting me during school vacations. She was very popular with them before—well, before. But there are a few new families who have come to Oakdale since—well, since."

"Before what? Since what?" If it was rude of Kate, she could not help it. It was all too mystifying.

"But that's just what I can't tell you, since Katherine hasn't. Only, your not knowing makes it a bit complicated. No, I'm not sure of that. It may make everything more simple, more natural. But tell me, can't you be friends with Elsie? She needs your friendship and companionship more than you can guess, my dear."

"I'm sorry. Perhaps we shall be friends yet. But she does act awfully *queer.* Oh, it's mean of me to talk about her so. Perhaps I've done something. Perhaps there's a reason."

"Well, she's a strange child. Strange! But she used to be different. I always thought she seemed a little lost and lonely, you know. That was mostly because of her mother—no mother at all, in reality. Just a butterfly. In spite of that Elsie was agreeable and tender once. Quite a dear. But since she has come to live with me she has been entirely a changed person. You must believe, though, Kate, that there is no more reason for her to be unfriendly toward you than there is for her to be unfriendly toward me. And I am speaking truly when I say there has hardly been a friendly moment between us since she came into my home. She is polite, beautifully polite. I suppose that absurd fashionable boarding school she was sent to taught her manners. But it goes no deeper. How do *you* feel about it? Is there anything unkind or wrong in the way I treat Elsie? Have you noticed anything in the brief time you have been here?"

Kate was amazed to have Aunt Katherine so appealing to her. All barriers were down between them. They were talking as two girls might, or two women.

"Nothing unkind, of course! I don't know how you could be kinder. But, Aunt Katherine, do you truly like Elsie? It may be that she *feels*, in spite of your kindness, that you just don't like her."

"Does it seem that way to you?"

"No—perhaps not. But there is something in your voice when you speak to her—a difference. I don't know how to express it. If you truly don't like her, perhaps you can't help showing it a little."

Aunt Katherine said no more for a while. But she was thinking. "It's queer," she said finally, "very queer, the way I am talking to you. I am treating you as though you were your mother almost. And you are like your mother, in deep ways. Only you are franker, more open. You say right out the things that she might think but wouldn't say. Well, and since I am saying things right out, too—I *don't* like Elsie. You are right there. I tried to. But I simply couldn't. She is too unnatural, too cold and heartless, and perhaps self-seeking. The irony of it is that she is all I have left to love, the only person in the world who needs me now—or, rather, the only person who will let herself use me. But I can't like her."

Kate was embarrassed at this revelation, and at the same time deeply sorry for her aunt. For the present the subject dropped between them.

*   *   *   *   *   *   *   *

In Boston Kate looked about her with the greatest interest as the car crept through the crowded business section. She had been in Boston before on brief holiday visits with her mother, stopping at little boarding houses, and spending most of the time in art galleries or the Museum or on trolley rides to places of historical interest. But now she was seeing it from a new angle, leisurely and in comfort. There was no jostling, no hurrying, no aching feet.

They drew up to a curb in Boylston Street. Timothy got out and came around for orders. "Go up and ask Mr. O'Brien to come down to the car, Timothy. Tell him I have only a minute."

Almost at once a spruce, energetic-looking young man stood at the car door, his straw hat in his hand.

"Wouldn't it be better to have our interview, no matter how brief, in my office, Miss Frazier?" he suggested deferentially.

Miss Frazier shook her head with decision. "No. I just want to ask you one question. Is there any news?"

Mr. O'Brien glanced toward Kate significantly.

"This is my niece," Miss Frazier informed him but not at all in the way of an introduction. "Tell me, have you the slightest news?"

"Nothing that is very certain. We have a new clue, perhaps. But I cannot go into that before your niece, Miss Frazier."

"Oh, this is not Elsie. It's another niece, a blood relation. And I do not intend to climb those stairs to your office. You can surely give me some hint."

"There is an elevator. You forget."

"No matter. I am not going up. Be quick, please. Naturally, I am impatient."

Kate was certainly catching a glimpse now of the bossy Aunt Katherine of tradition.

"Well, we just have an idea. We should like to know whether your other niece, Miss Elsie, ever comes into Boston alone. Has she been in this week, say?"

"Why, no. Certainly not. Bertha, her maid, is with her when I am not. She is a chaperon as well as a maid. I trust her. She happens to be a very remarkable woman for a servant."

"Miss Elsie does come in, then, without you sometimes? Is she planning to come soon again?"

"Why, yes. But what this has to do with the business I can't see. I'm sending her in to-morrow with her maid and Miss Kate to buy party frocks and see 'The Blue Bird.'"

"Excellent!" Mr. O'Brien seemed much pleased. "Will they go directly to the store?"

"Yes, Pearl's. A modiste on Beacon Street."

"Very good. May I have one word in your ear?"

"I see no reason." But Miss Frazier leaned a little toward the insistent young man while he lowered his voice so that Kate did not catch one word of what he said.

Her aunt laughed, amused apparently. "Much good that will do you. I have told you, Mr. O'Brien, there is not a chance in the world that Miss Elsie knows any more than we do."

"However, you do not object?"

"No. Except that it is a foolish waste of time."

"We shall not lose time through it, I assure you. Other members of my staff are working on other clues. Precious few there are, though."

"If that is all I will say 'good afternoon,' then." Miss Frazier settled back in her seat. "You will call me up, of course, the minute there is anything definite."

"Of course. But does Miss Elsie often answer the telephone?"

"Sometimes. Very seldom. I tell you, Mr. O'Brien, there is no rhyme or reason to your suspicions in that direction."

"Even so, Miss Frazier, I beg you to adjure Miss Kate here to secrecy. She should, on no condition, tell Miss Elsie one word she has heard."

Miss Frazier nodded, glancing at Kate. Kate's return look carried her promise. "I shall hope for something more definite when next I hear from you, Mr. O'Brien. Good afternoon. Home, Timothy."

Mr. O'Brien stood on the curb while the big car pulled out. There was a troubled, displeased expression on his face, Kate thought. She knew that he resented very much the interview not having been more private.

"Is he a detective?" she asked her aunt curiously.

"Yes, a private detective, and a very good one. But perhaps he is right, Kate, and you had better forget all about him. If he is doing the job I suppose he has a right to do it in his own way."

A private detective! And what had a detective to suspect of Elsie! But Kate took her aunt's hint and asked no more questions.

Their way home took them by the Green Shutter Tea Room, a quaint little place built by a stream in a grove of maples. The tables were set out under the trees. Aunt Katherine suggested that they stop. And when they were seated opposite each other at a little round green table, their order given, they smiled at each other contentedly, like friends of long standing.

CHAPTER IX
SOMETHING OF FAIRY IN IT

"You haven't told me a word about how you like the orchard house!" Aunt Katherine said. "Did you go all over it? The study is really the nicest room. Did you like that? And did you see your mother's old playroom?"

Kate hesitated to confess to her aunt that she had not been near the orchard house. It might involve Elsie too much. She remembered Elsie's plea last night. So she hesitated, feeling her cheeks redden. But after an instant she said, "I think I shall save it for a day when there isn't so much to do. It's a darling house, but I haven't been in."

"After the party on Thursday I am hoping that all your days here will be full of things to do, yours and Elsie's, too. She will begin to have the life of other girls again. For myself I have hardly cared a bit. I had rather grown away from my old friends, anyway, and larger interests, or at least more impersonal interests, have been absorbing me of late years. But now I'm pocketing my pride for Elsie's sake, and going more than halfway toward reconciliations.... Madame Pearl, the woman to whom I am sending you to-morrow for frocks, is an artist in her way. You two girls must choose dresses that not only become yourselves but go well together."

For Kate all the puzzling hints that ran through her aunt's conversation were forgotten in this new subject. "But Mother and I thought my pink organdie would do for a party, if you gave one. You haven't seen it. I shall wear it for dinner to-night."

"No, I haven't seen it, but I am sure it is very dainty and pretty. Even so, this is to be Elsie's first real party, and her first real party frock. And it will be more appropriate for you to have dresses that match in a way, or contrast with each other artistically. You *will* let me give you such a gift, won't you, Kate?"

There was surprising entreaty in Aunt Katherine's dark eyes, and fear, too. Would Kate be simply an echo of her mother? Would she rise up in pride and say, "No charity, thanks"?

Meanwhile, Kate was thinking rapidly. She had no idea whatever whether her mother would want her to accept a party frock from Aunt Katherine or not. But quickly she decided that her mother would want her to speak for herself now, that this was a matter between herself and her aunt.

"Of course I shall love to have a party dress," she exclaimed. "Oh, but you are good to me, Aunt Katherine! And it will be my first as well as Elsie's."

Miss Frazier flushed, pleasure all out of proportion to the event, seemingly, shining from her eyes. She said "Thank you, my dear," in as heartfelt accents as though Kate herself were the donor.

Kate laughed at that, her eyes crinkling, and after the laugh her mouth still stayed tilted up at the corners. "Oh, I'm so excited," she exclaimed. "But aren't you going to Boston with us, to Madame Pearl's, to help us choose?"

"No, I think not. Bertha has excellent taste, and Madame Pearl herself would not make a mistake. And I think that the more I am out of it the better the chance is that you and Elsie will find each other. A day together, shopping, lunching at my club, and seeing 'The Blue Bird' afterward ought to give two girls all the opportunity they need to get over any strangeness."

"'The Blue Bird'! Well, it's just as Mother said it would be, wonderful things galore! Oh, dear! I wish she could know this minute that I'm to see 'The Blue Bird'! We've read it, of course. But to see it! I shall write her again to-night—and the boys, too."

Kate was sitting with clasped hands, her hazel eyes narrowed and golden with light. She was almost little-girlish in her excitement and pleasure, and of course the corners of her mouth were uptilted at their most winged angle. Aunt Katherine, watching her, thought, "She is better than pretty, this grand-niece of mine. She is fascinating. Just to look at her stirs your imagination."

But she said, "Eat your toast before it is cold, I advise you. And don't neglect the marmalade. It is unusually good marmalade they serve here at the Green Shutter."

And so Kate came to earth. "But such a nice earth!" she said to herself.

Before they had finished their tea, Aunt Katherine rose to a pitch of confidences that surprised herself. But it was just exactly as though in Kate she had found a friend, a friend to whom she was able to open her heart. At this moment in her life Miss Frazier needed this sort of a confidante badly. They were talking about Elsie again and her coldness and indifference to Kate.

"There is one obvious explanation for it," Aunt Katherine said. "I can think of no other. She may be jealous. She may have been jealous from the first minute of your arrival."

Kate was too surprised to think at all. "Jealous—*of me?* Why?"

"That you might take her place with me, cheat her somehow of what she apparently considers hers. She sees, as you have guessed, that I do not like her. May she not be all the more jealous of you just because of that?"

"Oh, no, no, no." Kate was thinking clearly again. "She isn't horrid like that. I know it. She's too beautiful and lovely. There's something about her that makes any such idea just impossible. She mayn't like me, and I may be cross with her, but for all that—for all that I know she's not a *mean* person, Aunt Katherine."

Kate was amazed herself at having so suddenly become Elsie's champion. Loyalty to that strange girl had apparently been born in her all in a second. Or was it loyalty only to the comrade she had glimpsed flashingly, once in the mirror last night, and once in sunshine this morning? Whatever it was to, it was very real and staunch.

Aunt Katherine's face lightened remarkably. "You may be right, and I earnestly hope you are," she said. "For if Elsie were unfriendly toward you for any such reason—well, it would be the last straw, the very last."

As they spun along toward home through the cooling air, Miss Frazier's expression grew happier and happier. Kate had done for her what she could not do for herself: lightened real suspicions, and eased her heart.

It was almost dinner time when they arrived. If Kate was to don her pink organdie she would have to hurry. She raced up the stairs and found Bertha in her room waiting for her.

"You have only ten minutes, Miss Kate," she warned. "Your bath is set."

A glance showed Kate the pink organdie freshly pressed, crisp and cool, hung over a chair back, and the white slip to go under it on the bed. Her pumps were set down by the dressing table and some fresh stockings near on a stool. Two baths a day! How comfortable! Kate, still aglow with her afternoon, had quite forgotten her self-consciousness with this lady's maid.

"Has Miss Elsie dressed?" she asked.

Bertha answered rather worriedly: "No, and none of us have seen her all afternoon. I do wish she would come up. I can't think how she's been amusing herself, or where."

Kate herself began to wonder, when she had had her bath and was freshly dressed. "There's the gong!" she exclaimed.

But simultaneously with the note of the gong Elsie's door slammed and there she was in the bathroom door.

"I'm late," she called, but not at all ruefully. "No time to dress, Bertha. Hello, Kate."

"You'll have to wash your face, whether there's time or not," Bertha assured her. "And your hair, it's a sight! Where did you get like that?"

Elsie laughed, elfin laughter. "Never mind where. And you aren't my nurse. You're my tiring-woman. Bear that in mind, Mrs. Bertha."

Bertha's worried face changed into a beaming one. Elsie in such good spirits! That was the best that Bertha asked of life, Kate intuitively felt.

But it was true enough. Elsie very much needed washing and brushing. Her nose and forehead were beaded with little drops of perspiration, her cheeks were a burning red, as though she had been sitting over a fire, or perhaps long in the sun, and there were smudges of what looked like flour on chin and arms. As for her hair, it was all in little damp curls across her brow and over her ears: one side had come completely undone, and showered down on to her shoulder.

"I can't for the life of me see how you ever got in such a mess," Bertha murmured happily as she officiated in Elsie's hurried cleaning up. "You might just as well be a cook in a kitchen! But, oh, dear! What's that burn?"

"It is horrid, isn't it?" Elsie agreed.

"Well, I think you need a nurse more than a lady's maid! Did Julia let you get near the stove on this broiling day? Here's some olive oil."

After another minute of scurrying Elsie appeared in Kate's door. "It was nice of you to wait for me," she said. "But I'm afraid I've made you late."

Aunt Katherine lifted her brows when she saw Elsie still in her blue and white morning dress. But the fact that the girls had come in together, actually arm-in-arm, made up for much. In fact, it put Aunt Katherine into a light and gay mood. Things were beginning to go as she had planned now. At dinner she told Elsie about the party set for Friday night. And Elsie, who herself was in a gay spirit, thanked her aunt prettily for everything—the coming party, the promised frock, and the seats for "The Blue Bird."

"Why, she is a human being, after all," Kate admitted. "This morning and last night seems like some dream I had about her." And Kate opened her hazel eyes a little wider now as she looked at Elsie across the table. She was on the watch for the reappearance of the vanishing comrade.

That evening again Miss Frazier sent the girls to walk in the garden. She herself settled down in the big winged chair under her especial reading lamp and picked up "The King of the Fairies," which Kate had not forgotten to place there.

The orchard drew all Kate's attention once they were out in the growing starlight. She looked toward it often as they paced back and forth on the garden paths. At first she talked to Elsie about her afternoon, the ride, and the Green Shutter Tea Room. But Elsie, though she listened with interest, and even took pains to ask questions, in return gave Kate no information as to how *she* had spent the hours. Even so, Elsie was so completely changed that finally Kate had the hardihood to tell her laughingly about the light she had seen in the orchard house last night before falling to sleep.

"I am sure I saw the light. But of course I couldn't have heard the door," she finished. "That must have been imagination, for sound doesn't carry like that."

But at this mention of the orchard house Elsie's new manner fell from her as though she had dropped a cloak. She stiffened as they walked and her voice took on restraint.

"If you imagined the sound of the door, why wasn't the light imagination, too?" she asked reasonably. "Or it may have been fireflies in the trees. See them now."

It was true enough. Over in the orchard fireflies were twinkling, almost in clouds.

"It wasn't like firefly light, just the same."

"Well, you were almost asleep, weren't you? It was probably fireflies and sleepiness all mixed up."

Kate did not acknowledge that she was impressed by this reasoning. But deep in her mind she was.

"And you're not to tell Aunt Katherine about the light. Promise me that. She would go investigating then. You've got to promise."

Kate's quick temper flashed up and ruined the new relation between them at Elsie's brusque command.

"I haven't got to promise. Why do you think you can boss me like that?"

Elsie's answer to that was a tossed head. "I'm going in," she said shortly.

"*I'm* not." Kate sat down abruptly in a garden chair they were passing. When Elsie had gone on Kate bit her lip, hard, hard to keep back the tears. "Now I've spoiled everything," she accused herself bitterly. "Why did I have to go talking about the orchard house at all? Everything was so jolly, so right at last! Elsie was beginning to be more than decent. What an idiot I am!"

She leaned her head down upon the arm of the chair. Then the inner, more tranquil Kate came forward. "Think about the King of the Fairies," she said. "Look as he looked, see as he saw. Perhaps if you do, all this trouble will dissolve in light. Get above the quarrel."

And as she sat curled up there, she tried hard to follow the inner Kate's directions. She tried to look at the orchard with the different seeing. If she followed the King of the Fairies' directions, mightn't she see the *all* of things as the girl and boy on the fence had seen the all? She stayed very still, and watched, expectantly.

Elsie came back to her, silent as a shadow. It was almost as though she could read Kate's thoughts; for she knelt down by her on the dewy grass, and putting her face quite close to Kate's said in a low voice, but earnestly: "I'll tell you this much, Kate Marshall, *there is something fairyish about that little orchard house.* If things fairyish show to you around it or in it, it is because they *are there.* This is no lie. I cross my heart. But you aren't wanted there. And unless you are very mean you will keep your promise to me and not go near."

Then Elsie floated away, and was lost to Kate in the garden shadows, like a fairyish thing herself.

Kate started up. Had she dreamed Elsie's coming back, and her words? She had been in such a *different* state of mind trying to see as the King of the Fairies saw, that she hardly knew. Anyway, big girl of fifteen that she was, she began looking again toward the orchard house with deepened expectancy.

CHAPTER X
IN THE MIRROR

If Elsie had thought to tease or bewilder Kate in the garden last night by asserting that fairies actually had something to do with the orchard house she would have been disappointed now if she could read Kate's mind as she lay awake in the early morning. A sense of something exciting in the day had waked her before dawn. The excitement, of course, was the party frock that Aunt Katherine had promised her, and "The Blue Bird."

"I can hardly believe that I am going to have such a wonderful day," she thought. "Is it really happening to me? Will the morning ever come?"

She had no idea what time it was but she could see that the sky was beginning to lighten. She felt that she could never go to sleep again and she felt very hungry. Ah-ha! She remembered the gingerbread man under her pillow. She had put it there simply to hide it and meaning to get rid of it somehow without Elsie or Bertha seeing. She had not thought she would ever want to eat it! It was too childish. But now she pulled it out, and leaning up on her elbow ate every last crumb.

This elbow position brought the orchard into her view, or rather its growing outlines in the approaching dawn. She recalled last night and Elsie's emphatic assurance that fairies somehow had a hand in the mystery. Perhaps most other girls of fifteen would simply have laughed at Elsie and not for an instant accepted it as a possibility, fairies not entering into their scheme of things. But fairies did enter into Kate's scheme of things and always had. There she was different. But there was a reason for her difference.

When she was a little girl of seven she had seen what she thought was a fairy; and it had made such an impression on her mind that when she grew older and came to the age of doubt she simply went on knowing. She had seen what she had seen, and that was all there was to it. Moreover, her mother had seen it, too, or something like it. It was hardly likely that both of them could have been utterly deceived.

It happened when she and Katherine had gone for a walk on a June Saturday. They started very early in the morning and walked very far, for a seven-year-old. But it was Saturday and they were both free, Kate from the lessons which her mother set her, and Katherine from teaching. And it was June. So they did not seem to get tired a bit, but walked and walked, and explored. Toward noon they came to a high meadow hilltop. There they lay down, flat on their backs among the Queen Anne's lace, buttercups, and daisies, their arms across their eyes, their faces turned directly up toward the sun. It was luncheon time, but they did not care. The sunshine soaking into them and the smell of warm grass and earth were better than food.

They lay still for a long time, not even speaking to each other. Perhaps the little Kate slept. And they thought of getting up and starting for home only when the sun in the sky told Katherine that it must be past two o'clock.

Halfway down the hill pasture stood a little beach wood. They took their way through that because it looked so cool and inviting, and because Katherine knew there was a spring there among some rocks where they could get long, satisfying drinks of cold water. It was there they saw the fairy. They saw her just as they came out of the bright sunlight into the green, cool shade of the wood and stood above the water. She was at the other side of the spring facing them. She was looking down at her reflection in the water, not at all aware of their approach.

Kate saw her as a lovely girl in a floating green garment. Her feet and arms were bare and shining and it was their shining that made Kate know, even in that first instant before the fairy had glanced up, that she was unearthly. Kate and Katherine stood as still as the leaves on the trees in that still wood, awed and entranced. Then the little Kate whispered "Mother!" and pointed. At that whisper the fairy lifted her eyes. Kate saw the surprise in her eyes and a dawning—something; was it friendliness, or a smile? There was not time to know; for the fairy flashed backward and up on to a stone behind her across which the sunlight fell. And there she was lost in the sunlight. They simply could not see her any more.

But Kate had never forgotten that instant when they stood looking at the fairy while she was plain to view. And she had never forgotten the expression on her mother's face after the fairy had vanished. It was such a delighted expression, so startlingly *satisfied*.

But that night, in talking it over, it came out that mother and daughter had not seen exactly the same thing. Katherine was sure that the being who had stood looking down at the spring was taller than human, grander, with a more tranquil, noble face, And her garment, she said, was the colour of sunlight, not green at all. Little Kate protested that. No, she was just a slim girl and her garment was green. Why, Kate remembered exactly how it hung almost to her bare ankles, without fluttering or motion in that still wood. The golden gown Katherine had seen had blown back, she said, as in a strong wind, although she herself felt no breath of air.

The end of their discussion came to this. Katherine said it might be that the sun in the high meadow together with their having had no luncheon had made them see not quite true. When they came suddenly into the cool, green shaded wood out of the glare their eyes played them tricks. What seemed like a person standing above the spring may have been simply an effect of sunlight striking through leaves.

"You remember, don't you," Katherine had ended, "how she vanished into sunlight when you said 'Mother'? Well——"

And Katherine had left it at that. "Well——" But she had warned little Kate not to talk about it.

"People will think I had no business letting you go without luncheon so," she gave as her reason, laughingly.

But just because she had promised Katherine that she would not talk about having seen a fairy, Kate had thought about it all the more. And she never went into a cool wood out of hot sunlight without hoping to surprise a fairy again. What she had seen she had seen, and that was all there was to it!

So now to Kate the thought that fairies might somehow be connected with the little orchard house did not seem at all an impossibility. Elsie certainly had not acted or looked as though she were lying. And it was perfectly true that from the minute Kate herself had first caught sight of the orchard house she had felt that there was something very special about it—more special than just the fact that it was the house where her mother had been born and grown up and married. When Elsie called out "Fairies, beware! Orchard House, beware!" Kate had been pricked with the feeling of listening ears. She had felt somehow that the warning was truly heard and taken.

She stretched now to her full length between her scented sheets. "I do wish the dawn would hurry up and dawn!" she thought. "The minute it's a bit light enough I'll get up, take a cold bath, dress, and get out into the orchard. If fairies are there, dawn ought to be as easy a time to see them as any. I'll keep my promise about the key. But I've a perfect right in the orchard."

She fell asleep then and dreamed about the orchard house. The King of the Fairies was there, waiting for her on the doorstep. She sat down beside him and at once began to see things different, to see them, as the King of the Fairies said, "whole." There was a lot to the dream—colour, adventure, and music, and above all, the sight of things "whole." But Kate, when she woke, had quite lost it. The dream had become just tag ends of brightness left floating in her mind.

*   *   *   *   *   *   *   *

To her surprise morning was fully established, birds were singing in high chorus, and water was running loudly into the tub!

Bertha appeared in the bathroom door. "Miss Elsie got ahead of us," she informed Kate brightly. "She must have been quieter than a mouse to have had her bath and all and not waked you. Now I suppose she's out in the orchard or somewhere. It's a beautiful day."

Oh, well, Kate did not allow herself to be downcast at having missed dawn in the orchard. Not a bit of it. What a day it was to be! The frock, "The Blue Bird," the whole day in Boston with Elsie, and Aunt Katherine so friendly!

At her place at the little breakfast table under the peach tree she found a letter from her mother. She snatched it up and tore it open, hoping she could get at least the heart out of it before Aunt Katherine and Elsie should appear.

But she had hardly read the first sentence before Miss Frazier came out through the breakfast-room and Elsie floated from the direction of the orchard. Kate was too absorbed to be aware of the approach of either until she heard Elsie exclaim, "Letters! Oh, is there one for me?"

Aunt Katherine's tone was surprisingly sharp when she answered, "You never get letters, Elsie. You have hardly had one in the last year."

"That's unfair," Kate thought hotly. "Aunt thinks she's jealous even of my mail. And all the time she's probably expecting an answer to that special delivery she sent yesterday."

But in spite of the edge in Miss Frazier's voice Elsie apparently was not at all dashed. To Kate's curious eyes she looked just exactly as one might who had been skylarking with fairies in the orchard all early morning. She was ready to laugh, ready to talk, ready to be friendly. Kate was profoundly glad, for this kind of an Elsie argued well for the day they were to have in Boston together.

They went by train because Miss Frazier herself had uses for the car. Bertha was again dressed in her correct gray tailored suit. "Looking like an aunt herself," Kate thought. Kate wore the blue silk dress she had travelled in and the smart little hat that was really her mother's. The white linen would have done beautifully if they had not been going to the theatre; but even though they were to sit in the balcony—seats were sold out so far ahead that this was the best Aunt Katherine had been able to do for them—Kate thought the white linen would hardly be appropriate for that, and Bertha had agreed with her. Elsie, when she appeared, quite took Kate's breath away. She was so lovely, but so much older looking than she had been in her house clothes. She was dressed in a straight little three-piece silk suit of olive green. The rolling collar was tied by a jaunty orange bow, and on the low belt of the dress the same colour was embroidered in a conventional flower pattern. The coat hung loosely and very full, hooked together only at the collar. The hat was a limp dark brown straw with olive-green and orange embroidery all around the crown. Elsie had pinned her curls up over her ears, and her hair was a soft crushed aura under the hat. She looked very much like a city girl but as though the city might have been New York or Paris rather than Boston.

Kate gasped a little, and in her secret heart was very glad she herself had decided on her silk. For a little while she was constrained with Elsie, as though Elsie had in fact become older suddenly just because she looked older.

As they came through the gates at their terminal in Boston Kate noticed a young man in a slouch brown hat, a polka-dotted brown tie, and very shining pointed brown shoes, standing about as though expecting someone to meet him from the train on which they had come in. Perhaps Kate noticed him so particularly because he seemed to be noticing them so particularly, especially Elsie. For the first time that morning she remembered Mr. O'Brien, the detective. Was this one of his men, and was he going to "shadow" them to-day? Kate was sure of it when out of the tail of her eye she saw him wheel and follow at a little distance as they moved toward the taxi stand. He stood prepared to take the next cab that should move into position as theirs moved out. Kate hardly understood her own emotions at that moment. Her cheeks were hot and her knees shook a little. She was resentful for Elsie. Why was she being shadowed by a detective as though she were a criminal? Why had Aunt Katherine let this happen?

Madame Pearl's establishment was a narrow three-story house on Beacon Street. "Madame Pearl" was engraved on a plate above the bell, nothing more. A daintily capped and aproned maid answered their ring. She knew their names before they had given them.

"It is the Misses Frazier," she said, speaking with a distinct accent. "You have an engagement, and Madame Pearl is expecting. Please come this way."

The front door opened directly into a long narrow room, panelled in ivory, decorated with wreathed cupids and flowers. The floor was cool gray and the hangings at the long windows at the end of the room were gray, too, silvery. But under their feet were warm-coloured Persian rugs of the most beautiful shades and designs. There were little tables in the room with magazines and books scattered on them, a few easy chairs, and two long divans. In one corner by the window there was an exquisite little writing desk of Italian workmanship. On this stood a vase of very red roses.

Kate glanced about with surprised eyes. But Elsie, who had been here before with Aunt Katherine, nonchalantly followed the maid who was guiding them. Kate had expected to find herself in a shop. But there was no evidence of things for sale here. And they had an appointment! Whoever heard of having an appointment in a shop?

The maid stood back at the foot of a narrow spiral staircase at the back of the room. The girls and Bertha ascended.

Still no sign of a shop, or dresses for sale. This long upper room was simply a boudoir with chaises-longues, mirrors, and flowers. Madame Pearl swept to meet them. She was a regal little lady in trailing gray chiffon. The gown had long flowing sleeves that just escaped the floor. Miss Frazier had told Kate at breakfast that morning that Madame Pearl was really a Russian princess who had escaped at the time of the Revolution and in just a few years had made a fortune with this shop. Her real name was Olga Schwankovsky. So Kate looked at her with intense curiosity now. But where was the shop?

"Miss Frazier has telephoned," Madame Pearl said in the sweetest of voices and almost perfect accent. "You young ladies are to have party dresses, your first party dresses. Very simple, very chic, youthful. We must not hurry but give time to it and consideration. If you will be so kind as to come this way——"

"This way" was all down the room to a wider alcove, walled on the street by big plate-glass windows and on the two other sides by huge, perfect mirrors.

There Madame Pearl asked them to be seated. She herself sat comfortably among cushions on a little lounge. She inquired as to their favourite colours. From that the conversation expanded to their other tastes, to books, music. Elsie told about their plan for the afternoon.

"You are to see 'The Blue Bird'!" Madame Pearl exclaimed. "That will be an experience. I myself saw it when I was about your age—its first production at the Moscow Art Theatre. I had never dreamed anything could be so beautiful. You will think so, too." Then she added, sighing a little, "But it cannot be quite the same. Stanislavsky produced it as it never could be produced by another. It was superb."

"You saw it, there, when it was given in Moscow that first time?" Elsie breathed, sitting on the very edge of her chair, her cheeks pink with excitement. "That was wonderful. I know, for my fa——" She stopped, bit her lip, and continued: "Someone showed me photographs of the stage sets and costumes once. I am wondering if it will be anything like that here."

"I don't know," Madame Pearl replied. "But I tell you frankly I am not going to see. For the memory of our Art Theatre production is too vivid for me to want to expose it to any comparison. It was done with a richness, a depth, a true sense of mysticism—— What shall I say? It was so free of sentimentality. I confess I do not care to see it attempted again. It had an effect on me, that play. An effect that is lasting, that runs through—how shall I say?—my life."

Elsie nodded and looked at Kate. She said, "Yes, we understand. 'The King of the Fairies' is like that, too."

Kate's heart leapt. At last those two girls had met face to face, comrades on common ground.

"'The King of the Fairies,'" Madame Pearl murmured, reflectively. "Ah, yes. I have heard of that book. Published last year. Very beautiful, I have heard. And literary people are surprised because it is so popular. They alone, when they discovered it, expected to appreciate it and enjoy. They are a little annoyed that children and simple people and the unliterary love it, too, that it is a 'best seller.' I have guessed, though I have not yet read it, that that book must tap some deep wells of truth that all humanity knows, even the simple. I have a theory about art——"

There the beautiful voice ceased abruptly. Madame Pearl rose, smiling enigmatically. "This is not choosing frocks, is it?" she said. "But while we have chattered I have studied your types. I have not been idle. Shall we begin with the one of which I am the least sure? That is Miss Kate. We may have to try several frocks before we are suited for you. But I think we shall begin with an orange crêpe."

Madame Pearl touched a button in the wall and almost instantly a maid appeared, not the one who had answered the door, but identically dressed. She was young and pretty and very quick in all her motions. Kate found a screen placed around her almost before she knew what was happening. It was a light folding screen made of gray silk and bamboo and embroidered with oriental flowers. Bertha hastened to disrobe her. Then she came forth and stood ready to try on before one of the huge mirrors.

Panels in the wall were slid back and the little maid brought the dresses from their hiding places one by one. Bertha and the little maid slipped them over her head, fastened them, turned her around lightly by the shoulders. Then everyone looked at Madame Pearl. She was sitting on her couch again, her eyes intent. She studied Kate as an artist studies his picture. And to every frock, when it was on and Kate had been turned quite around once or twice, she shook her head decidedly. None of them, not one would do.

Kate herself could not see why. There was not one that was positively unbecoming, and three or four had been quite lovely. She was growing dazed and tired. The sparkle and colour of the frocks heaped about her on chairs and thrown over the screen was almost too much for her eyes. She thought of the Arabian Nights and imagined herself a young princess of Arabia being decked for her wedding. But even as the corners of her mouth lifted with this dream she was startled by an exclamation from Madame Pearl.

"At last! It is perfect!"

Kate turned to herself in the mirror.

But was it Kate Marshall at all? She scarcely knew.

The frock was yellow, of softest satin, the color of a crocus. At the rounded neck it was gathered softly to a narrow border of tiny pearl-white and blue blossoms made in satin. At the low waistline the satin was gathered again at a girdle of the same exquisitely fashioned flowers, four wreaths of them loosely twined. The skirt swung out from this girdle very full and straight, stopping just a little above the ankles, quite the longest skirt Kate had ever had. The border of the skirt was cut in deep, sharp scallops showing an underskirt below of foaming, creamy lace.

"Do you like it?" Madame Pearl asked, interestedly. Kate was looking at herself without speaking.

"I couldn't help liking it," Kate replied. "It's beautiful. But—it doesn't look exactly as though we belonged—it and I together! It is fluffy! So delicate!"

"That's the fault of your hair, the short bob," Madame Pearl assured her. "There must be a cap." She gave directions to the maid. "The silver cap with the star points. Yes, the one from Riis's. Deep cream stockings. And the pumps—but I see you know which pumps that frock must have yourself. I think they will fit, too. Fetch them."

The maid whisked away to return in a minute with silk stockings, satin slippers, and a silver cap.

"Your feet first," Madame Pearl said, quite excitedly. "The cap we will leave for the finishing touch. Then you shall see."

Again, almost in a daze, Kate vanished behind the painted screen accompanied by both Bertha and the maid. Each of them dressed a foot, and it was done in a minute. The pumps were an exact fit. They were creamy satin embroidered in deeper creamy-coloured flowers. At the side of each a small diamond-shaped crystal buckle caught the light in many facets. The heels were low.

Kate was troubled. "My aunt is only giving me the frock," she said. "She didn't mention slippers and things. I've some perfectly good black patent-leather pumps, anyway."

"Black pumps! With that frock!"

Madame Pearl gazed at her in horror. Bertha hurriedly interposed, "Miss Frazier impressed it on me that the costumes were to be complete."

Then Madame Pearl arose from the couch and herself set the silver cap on Kate's head. It was a saucy affair fashioned in crisp silver lace with five star points radiating from its crown. The cap was indeed the finishing touch. It accomplished almost a transformation.

"Why, I'm *pretty*, awfully pretty!" Kate exclaimed to herself, gazing into the mirror. But then more modestly, she added, "Any one would be in that fascinating cap."

So Kate was ready for the party! Let it come!

And now it was Elsie's turn. But Madame Pearl had no trouble in fitting Elsie to just the right frock. In fact, she had decided which it must be in the first minutes while they sat discussing "The Blue Bird." Elsie was not "difficult." Madame Pearl whispered to the maid, who scurried away. She returned bearing over her arm a cloud of green chiffon. While Kate was being dressed behind her screen Elsie was put into this green creation behind another similar screen. She appeared before Kate was done.

Her frock was simplicity itself, just straight lengths of green chiffon falling straight away from her slim shoulders. As she moved back and forth in front of the mirror her draperies floated about her like filmiest clouds. When she stood still they fell straight and sheer almost to her ankles. Madame Pearl signalled and the maid took the pins from Elsie's curls and they tumbled, a shower of sunlight.

The effect was perfect. Madame Pearl breathed softly: "I am satisfied. Exquisitely." She determined that white kid sandals, sandals in the Greek style, were the footwear the frock required. She had them, too, stored somewhere behind those secret panels. The maid hurried off, and Elsie in preparation for her return slipped off the black patent-leather sandals she was wearing, and out of her stockings.

At the same time Madame Pearl moved to the big windows. "The light is glaring," she murmured, "and it is unreasonably hot." Untying a cord at the side of the sash she let down green inner blinds. Elsie rose, and stood in her bare feet facing herself meditatively in the mirror. At that instant Kate came from behind her screen.

"Oh!" It was almost a shriek. Kate actually reeled against Bertha who was following her and clutched for support. Bertha led her to the couch. "Water, a glass of cold water quickly," Madame Pearl commanded the little maid. Elsie ran to Kate and knelt before her, taking her hands. "Kate, Kate," she called as though Kate were running away from her.

But Kate was not a girl to faint easily. She straightened up now and took a deep breath. "It's only the way you looked in the glass, Elsie," she explained, shakily. "The room just went spinning when I saw you."

"'The way she looked in the glass!'" Madame Pearl cast a hurried glance toward the big mirror that now reflected only Kate's array of discarded dresses, a few tables and chairs.

But Kate explained further, looking at Elsie wanly: "You were the fairy—the fairy that Mother and I saw by the pool that day. You were the fairy exactly, even the expression on your face when you looked at me! And the green light——"

Madame Pearl laughed. "The green light is only because I pulled the blind. But you are right, Miss Elsie does look exactly like some fairy, some wood fairy. Perfection."

"No, not some fairy, *the fairy*. I have remembered perfectly."

Madame Pearl spoke to Bertha aside, but Kate heard well enough. "It was the heat, and she was tired from trying on. She ought to lie down." Then she turned her attention to Elsie's sandals.

But Elsie kept looking back over her shoulder at Kate, resting on the sofa—questioningly. She was speculating: "Had Kate taken her hint of fairies in the orchard house seriously? Was it so much on her mind that she was imagining things? Or had Kate once really seen a fairy, and Elsie in the mirror had reminded her?"

When they left the shop and stood on the step looking about for a taxi Elsie asked Kate eagerly, "Did you really see a fairy once? Where? When?"

"Yes, Mother and I. But we both saw it differently. And now—now, how could it have been a fairy? Why, it was *you*. But I promised Mother not to talk about it."

At the mention of Kate's mother the cold look came back to Elsie's face. She turned away with feigned indifference while Bertha lifted her hand to summon a taxi.

CHAPTER XI
KATE TAKES THE HELM

But the taxi driver Bertha had signalled shook his head, giving a sidewise jerk toward the back of his cab to indicate that he had a fare. There was the young man of the brown hat and polka-dotted tie looking away as though he was not one bit aware of them and smoking a cigarette.

"Well, why do they stand still, then!" Bertha complained. "How could I know!"

Almost at once, however, another taxi came cruising up the hill, and they were soon in, whirling away toward Miss Frazier's club. It was now almost one o'clock, and they were quite ready for luncheon.

Though Kate did not actually lean out to see whether the detective's taxi was following, she felt quite sure that it was. "And he'll be wherever we go all day," she reflected. "What does he expect us to do—or Elsie, rather? What *could* she do with Bertha and me along, anyway? It's all just too curious! And I don't like it a bit. It makes me angry for Elsie. It isn't fair to her! I wonder what Mother and the boys would think if they knew I was riding around Boston to-day, buying gorgeous clothes, conversing with princesses, almost fainting, and being shadowed by a detective!

Both girls, lunching in Miss Frazier's club, felt themselves quite emancipated, really adult! Elsie wrote out their orders on a little pad tendered by a gray-clad waitress, and acted hostess throughout. Kate very much admired her worldly air, her poise and decision, and the way she knew the French names for things. Apparently she was quite accustomed to such complicated menus. Kate was proud of Elsie, proud and stirred. Aunt Katherine herself could not have conducted things better.

They discussed Madame Pearl and her establishment. They were both enchanted by her, and full of surmises about her life. Miss Frazier had told them that people knew very little about Madame Pearl's experiences during the Revolution and her escape, because she meant to keep out of the papers. That was why she had taken the name Madame Pearl, and did not want to be known as a princess at all, except to a few trusted customers, or rather patients.

"She prescribes clothes just as a doctor prescribes pills, Aunt Katherine says," Elsie remarked, laughing.

"I think my dress is too wonderful," Kate sighed. "But do you know I am afraid Mother won't want me to wear it to high-school dances next winter, if I go to any. She will say it's too grand, I'm sure."

In time, however, they left the topic of clothes and launched into discussion of "The Blue Bird." Both had read it, but in quite different ways. Kate had read for the story, and Elsie to fit it to the photographs she had seen of its first production in Moscow. In fact, this was typical of these two girls. They had enthusiasm for the same things, but approached them from different angles. That was why, when they found themselves talking freely, the air fairly sparkled between them. They opened new avenues of thought to each other, took each other's old ideas and spun them like balls, showing new sides and colours. They were animated. They leaned toward each other over the table, their faces alive and bright with thinking. Bertha remained mostly silent, enjoying her luncheon and the interested and appreciative glances that were turned from every direction upon her charges.

Luncheon went on slow feet because of conversation's wings. But they did not in any way neglect it. It was a most delicious meal, and quite a complicated one, because Miss Frazier had given Elsie carte blanche and told her to make it just as splendid as she pleased. After the ice they had a demitasse. Neither of the girls was accustomed to coffee, but this was a special day and they would do special things. Besides, the waitress seemed to expect it of them. It tasted horrible. But each made a brave effort and drank down the tiny portion without grimacing.

Now for the theatre!

At the door of the club a footman summoned a taxi for them. As Kate went down the steps and got in she looked all about for signs of the detective but saw none. However, they were in a crowded section, taxis and autos moving in two rivers, one north, one south, and the sidewalks were two more rivers—rivers of human beings. That polka-dotted young man might well have his eye on them from some station in that flow of life and Kate never be aware.

Elsie had the theatre tickets in her purse, and took them out now to be sure about them. "They're in the third row in the first balcony," she said. "Aunt Katherine thought they weren't very good, but I am sure they are. Why, it will be even better than as though we were 'way up front downstairs. We will get all the effects better. Don't you think so?" But she asked a trifle anxiously, as though trying to console herself.

Kate agreed, though to speak truth she knew very little indeed about the theatre and could hardly be considered a judge in any way. Both girls were glowing with anticipation and excitement. Kate felt that it was all simply too wonderful to be true. Her heart was almost breaking with happiness—at least, that is what she told herself was the matter with it. It certainly was pounding.

But arrived in the palace of gold decoration and purple plush which was the theatre, and ushered to their seats, there was an unpleasant surprise. One of the seats was directly behind a large ornate post! Whoever sat there would have to do a great deal of craning and stretching to see the stage at all, and not for one instant would she be able to see its entirety.

"Don't you bother," Bertha reassured them, concealing her own deep disappointment. "Of course I shall sit there. It's only a pity it's between you."

Now Elsie showed a new side of her character to Kate, and a side that she had not suspected. "Don't be silly," she told Bertha emphatically—but not rudely, merely affectionately—"Of course we shall take turns. I shall have the post for half the time and you the other. But it's mean, just the same."

"And I, too—I shall certainly take my turn," Kate threw in. "But I think it is mean, and a cheat, too!"

"No, you are the guest," Elsie said firmly. "You are to sit at the end and stay there. Go in now and I'll follow."

But Kate did not pass in. She stood frowning. "It isn't fair," she insisted. "They had no business to sell Aunt Katherine that seat."

Bertha shrugged. "Of course it's unfair," she whispered, "but there's nothing to do about it." She was bothered by the attention they were beginning to attract. She wished Kate would go in and sit down.

"Then we ought to complain," Kate insisted, still blocking up the aisle.

"To whom?" Bertha asked. Her tone said *she* would have nothing to do with it.

Elsie murmured quickly, "Oh, let's not," and gave Kate a slight push. She, too, was conscious of their conspicuous situation. "*I couldn't.*"

Kate, too, knew that they were attracting the attention of many people. All the more she was determined not to accept the injustice of that post seat meekly. They were early; the curtain would not go up for ten minutes. The orchestra was only just coming into the pit.

"You go in and sit down. But give me the ticket stubs. I'll make them fix this up." Kate did not whisper or even lower her voice. She spoke calmly, with assurance. Underneath she was as diffident as the other two, but hers was not a nature to tolerate such injustice supinely.

Elsie, with one quick, surprised glance, thrust the stubs into this country cousin's hand, and Kate was off up the steep aisle, bent on business. When she had pushed her way through the incoming crowds out into the upper foyer the first thing she saw was the detective, leaning against the wall trying to look unconcerned and as though he belonged there. In spite of the crowds their eyes happened to meet. Kate's cool look said, "So you are here." Then she turned away and fought her passage down the stairs.

The young man scowled. Well, this was not the niece he was to watch. She had light curls, and his chief had said she would be wearing a green silk suit. Even so this bobbed-haired one was of the party. He was troubled by her movements. What was she leaving her seat for? Where was she going? He really ought to find out, but, on the other hand, if he forsook his post here he might miss Miss Elsie if she should come out. No, he must stay, but it was annoying all the same.

At the box office they were turning people away. "No seats left," Kate heard on every side. But that did not stop her. "They can put a chair in the aisle," she thought. "They *must* do something. People should have what they pay for."

But the man at the ticket window gave her no hope. "All sold out," he assured her before she had had time to say a word. When he heard her complaint he merely said, "Well, we'll give you your money back. I could sell that post seat a hundred times over in the next five minutes. All you need is to *lean* a little. Where's your stub?"

"I don't want the money," Kate protested. "I want to see the play. It was a cheat, selling a seat like that. I want another one. In fact, I want three other seats, for we have to sit together."

The man laughed, much amused at that. And several by-standers laughed, too. Kate's cheeks fired.

"Where can I find the manager?" she asked, straightening her spine and looking hard at the amused young man.

The man strangled his laugh and pointed across the lobby to a door marked "Private." "There, if he's in. Much good it'll do you."

As Kate left the window and crossed to the door indicated she heard several titters. That made her determination deeper. She knocked firmly right in the middle of the word "Private."

As she got no answer to her knocking she followed her usual course when uncertain, or embarrassed—abrupt action. In this instance she simply opened the door and stepped in. She did this in exactly the way she often spoke when she had no intention of speaking. A man turned from a window where he was leaning looking down into the crowded street watching the people flooding to "The Blue Bird." He was a youngish man with nice lines around his eyes, smiling lines. But the eyes were very keen. Whether he was truly the manager or not Kate never learned, but he was manager enough for her purposes. She told him her grievance. He listened respectfully without a word until she had finished. Then, still without a word to her, he took up a telephone instrument from his desk and spoke briskly into it: "Box office, any seats left?" he asked. "Good, that's fine. Give the young lady who was at your window a minute ago one in the lower left." He hung up and turned to Kate.

"The house is sold out," he informed her in a voice that was fairly jubilant. "And they said it couldn't be done in the States in summer!" She felt that he wanted to dance and was constrained only by her presence. "All except a few box seats. They come too high. You can get yours now at the office all right. I've fixed it."

But Kate did not move to go. "There are three of us," she explained. "We have to stay together. We are with a chaperon. You hung up before I could tell you."

The manager was dashed. He had expected gratitude. "With a chaperon? Why isn't she here fixing things instead of you, then?" he asked with reason.

"Well, she didn't like to. She was willing to sit behind the post. She's really my cousin's maid, but my aunt lets her chaperon us."

"Oh, I see." There was something of humorous admiration in the manager's voice now. He liked Kate's spirit. He snatched up the telephone again. "Three seats for that lady just mentioned," he commanded into it. "Front ones."

Then Kate did thank him and smiled—her peculiar, charming smile. He responded to it with a beam of his own. But her last words were, "It was a cheat, wasn't it, selling that post seat to anybody."

His reply was simply "Rather!" as he held the door for her. She had read enough to know by his use of that word that he was English. He had spoken his "rather" in the most natural, sincere way possible.

The box-office man eyed her with respect. "Never thought you'd turn the trick," he said, admiringly. But Kate did not deign to answer. Suddenly she felt her conspicuousness too keenly. She took the tickets he offered her and fled away up the stairs, not looking at any one.

In the upper foyer the detective was on the watch for her. He sighed with relief when she appeared and vanished again through the swinging doors into the balcony. Well, his "party" was safe now until after the play. It was unfortunate that he had not been able to secure a seat inside where he could keep his eye on them directly. When the curtain went up he would slip in and stand in the back, of course. After all, things were pretty satisfactory. They certainly couldn't escape his attention now. So far their doings had been innocent enough, all except that little excursion of the bobbed-haired one.

Had she taken a note to someone? Perhaps he had been foolish not to follow her.

"Seats in a box! Oh, Kate, how did you ever!" Elsie looked at Kate with sincerest admiration shining in her eyes, and Kate felt for ever repaid for all her effort. If Elsie had acquitted herself well at luncheon, Kate had surely acquitted herself well here. They were equals. Comrades?

An usher hurried toward them as they came out into the aisle. "The curtain is about to go up," she warned. She felt, perhaps, that they had already made too much disturbance.

"Yes, but we have seats down in a box," Kate said with composure. The usher reached her hand for the tickets. "This way, then. There are stairs behind these curtains. If you hurry you'll be there before the lights go out."

"Ha, ha, Mr. Detective!" Kate laughed to herself as she felt her way down the narrow, velvet-carpeted stairs. "You are losing us now. You'll watch up there in vain."

Their seats were quite perfect, almost on the stage, three chairs in the very front of the best box in the house, three throne-like chairs with gilded arms and cushioned backs!

"We ought to be more dressed," Bertha whispered, a little uneasily, as in their conspicuous position she felt that the eyes of the whole great audience were upon them. But Elsie laughed softly. "Who cares!" she exclaimed. "And won't Aunt Katherine be surprised when she hears of all this state!"

Music. The asbestos curtain rolling up, revealing night-coloured velvet curtains with a huge gold shield. Lights out. The two girls, recently so estranged, were for the hours of this play closest sisters. In Fairyland all are friends. They gripped hands. Soon they simply sat close together, arm-in-arm, entranced. The theatre, the huge audience, dissolved for them in mist. The stage was not a stage. They were moving with Mytil and Tyltyl through frightening or lovely or saddening scenes, all equally enthralling. They were moving bodiless. They *were* Tyltyl and Mytil.

Not until the very last minute of the play, when the night-coloured curtains had drawn together for the last time and the blue bird was at large again, perhaps somewhere in the upper reaches of the gilded theatre, did the girls again take up their habitations in their own minds and bodies. They looked at each other then and sighed, waking as from a dream they had shared. Bertha was quite pale with emotion and surreptitiously wiping away her tears.

The first waking thought that Kate had was gratefulness that Bertha had seen the play as it ought to be seen and not cut in two by a post, since she cared for it so much.

All three were almost silent on the journey to the station, wrapped in the afterglow of the play's thraldom. But just outside the gates of the train shed Elsie looked all about and asked a question: "That young man in the polka-dotted tie seems to have disappeared," she observed. "He was here when we came, outside of Madame Pearl's in that taxi, in the hallway to the club and upstairs at the theatre. What's happened to him now?"

"Oh, did you notice him, too?" Kate asked, surprised. "And in the club? I missed him there. How did he get in?"

"He was talking to the telephone girl and watching us while we had lunch. I saw through the door. He acted like a detective, or something. I was going to point him out to you, and then every time I got interested in what we were saying and forgot. What do you suppose he was doing?"

Kate was suddenly embarrassed. She knew very well what he was doing, but of course she was bound not to tell.

"He acted like a detective," Elsie said, musingly. "Just exactly the way they act in books."

"Yes. And we might have been thieves, or something," Kate took it up.

But at her words Elsie stiffened. Although Kate at the minute was not looking at her she *felt* the stiffening. And when they were established in their coach and Kate did turn to look at Elsie she saw at once that the comrade had vanished again! What *had* she done? And how could she bear it after this perfect day? Oh, no, it was not to be borne. Things couldn't happen like that. She leaned toward Elsie and spoke quickly, urgently but softly.

"Don't get icy again," she pleaded. "If I've offended you, I truly don't know how. And we've had such a splendid day of it. Deep down everything seems to be all right with us. It's only on top things keep going wrong. Don't look like that. Don't."

But Elsie did not respond to Kate's pleading. She kept on looking "like that" and merely commented coldly, "You do say such queer things. I don't know what you mean."

And from then on Elsie, dropping all her city bearing, curled one foot up under her on the car seat, turned her shoulder to Kate, leaned her chin on her hand, and gazed out of the window. Kate sat biting her lips with clutched hands. After a while, when she realized that Elsie's "cold shoulder" was to be permanent, she got up and crossed the aisle to sit by herself at a window.

"Why am I not furious with her?" she asked herself. "She has no right to treat me like that! And I am angry, of course. But I'm not *very* angry. Why am I not very angry?"

The conclusion she finally arrived at was that she couldn't be very angry until she understood what it was all about. There was a mystery that needed solving. Kate felt herself destined to solve it. There was an elation in that prospect that bore her up above the moment's worries and confusions. "If you're going to live you've got to be willing to suffer," she told herself sententiously. "And certainly I am living!" Then her eyes crinkled into their nicest Chinese smile. For Kate was perfectly capable of being amused at herself.

CHAPTER XII
THE SPECIAL DELIVERY

Miss Frazier approved, and was even delighted with the frocks when she came up to view them after breakfast next morning.

"Shall we try them on for you?" Kate offered eagerly.

"No, I don't believe so. I can trust Madame Pearl, I am sure, to say nothing of you girls yourselves! And there is a lot to be done now to get ready for the party."

Miss Frazier was moving and speaking in suppressed excitement, any one could see that. This party to her was to be a significant moment in her own life as well as in the girls'!

"What can we do?" Kate asked.

"You may help me to decorate the drawing-room and hall. If I engage a professional person he will simply load the whole place with flowers in a set and stuffy way. Besides, this is an informal party, and we want the decorations to be very simple and unstudied." Then Miss Frazier added with a twinkle in her eye, "That's why we must study very hard and fuss and consult."

Both girls laughed at that.

"I'm expecting a man now to help Timothy move the furniture back for dancing. As soon as they are done we can begin. The dresses are charming, and I congratulate you."

Since getting into the train the afternoon before the comrade in Elsie had not been visible. The girls had spoken to each other only in monosyllables and with eyes usually averted. Almost as though they had agreed upon it, however, they played up a little in the presence of their aunt. She had been so kind to them and counted so much on the day together to have made them friends, they had not the heart to let her see just how things stood between them. So at dinner they had told her of the day's adventures vivaciously, dwelling most on their reactions to "The Blue Bird" and the episode of the post. For some reason Elsie did not mention the young man who had shadowed them in such an unshadowy way. That omission surprised Kate and gave her pause. What did such reticence mean? Aunt Katherine had been much diverted by Kate's account of her interview with the box-office clerk and the manager. Her comment had been, "You are a Frazier, Kate! You have a *spine*. I imagine the manager sensed that."

After dinner the three had settled to a quite exciting game of Mah Jong. No need for Elsie and Kate to pretend friendliness then, for the game took all their attention, and they could forget each other as persons. After that there was a brief stroll in the garden, Aunt Katherine walking between the girls, their arms drawn through hers. It had all seemed very peaceful and congenial. But there had been no "good-nights" upstairs, though in accordance with Aunt Katherine's will the doors stood open between the two bedrooms.

So now, when Aunt Katherine left to attend to the moving of the furniture, Kate turned to Bertha and said, "I shall be in the garden over by the Dentons' hedge, writing letters. Will you call me when Miss Frazier is ready, Bertha?"

Without a glance at Elsie she picked up her pad and hurried out. She hoped that Elsie realized she was avoiding using the sitting-room and the desk they were supposed to share; and she would not have minded knowing that Elsie's conscience bothered her about it. But if it did, Elsie gave no sign. She herself simply turned away about some business of her own.

There was so much for Kate to tell her mother in this letter that was interesting and wonderful! First, of course, there was Madame Pearl and her most unique shop that didn't look like a shop a bit. She must describe the frocks they had chosen, or rather that Madame Pearl had chosen for them; Kate realized now that they themselves had done no choosing at all. Then dining in the luxurious club—she would describe that in detail. She had never in her life had quite such a stimulating conversation with any one before as that conversation at luncheon. She recalled it now as an hour during which she had *thought*, and thought rapidly, and expressed her thoughts to an attentive listener who in her turn *thought* and came back at her in a most provocative manner. Ideas had spun in the air between them like iridescent bubbles, changing colour as they turned and you viewed different sides of them. The truth about that was that two most congenial minds had discovered each other, and that is as exciting an adventure as there is in the world, and not at all an ordinary one. The thing that gave this experience its final tang was that the two minds, though comprehending each other perfectly, worked entirely differently. It followed that for each other they had great discoveries and surprises. Together they danced as one in figures new to both!—Of course, Kate could not tell her mother exactly this, but she could tell her enough so that she would understand a little what had happened. But she must begin.

Instead, unhygienically, she sucked the end of her pencil.

Would Mother approve of her having accepted the party frock? That bothered her a little. Knowing Aunt Katherine now she understood her mother much less than ever before on these points. The dress must have cost—no, she would not imagine what it must have cost since Aunt Katherine had told her not to give that end of it a thought. Still, she would describe the dress to Mother, and she could come to conclusions for herself.

"Dearest Mother":—Oh, there was so much, so very much, it was quite hopeless to write! There was the fairy in the glass. That must be told first. There was not the slightest doubt in Kate's mind that the two were exactly the same, the fairy in the woods that day and the reflection of Elsie in the mirror at Madame Pearl's. But what its explanation could be was unthinkable. At the time the little Kate had seen the fairy in the woods, Elsie was only a little girl of her own age. How, then, had Kate seen her as she would look eight years later in a mirror in a Boston shop? It was such an unanswerable question that Kate's mind turned away from it. Still, not for one minute did she doubt that the two visions had been exactly the same. What would Katherine make of it?

"Hello. Good morning." Jack Denton, in white flannels, tall and athletic, was standing the other side of the hedge, swinging his tennis racket and smiling a friendly, frank smile. "Excuse me, but you're Miss Kate Marshall, aren't you? My sister and I are coming to the party in your honour to-night. I'm Jack Denton, and Rose will be out in a minute. If you'll play a set with us I'll call up another fellow and make doubles."

Kate jumped up, delighted. She went to the wall. "Good morning," she said. "I was just beginning a letter. But I'd love to play—that is, for a little while, till Aunt Katherine needs me. But why don't we just shout for Elsie? She likes tennis, I know, and Aunt Katherine says she plays wonderfully."

But Jack's expression had changed queerly. He grew slightly red and avoided looking directly at Kate. "No need to get any one yet," he objected. "Heaven knows when Rose will be out. She's awfully pokey—slow. Let us begin just by ourselves till she does appear, anyway. Can you jump? Here's a hand."

But Kate shook her head. "No, thanks. I don't think I'll play, after all. I may be called any minute to help Aunt Katherine, and besides—besides, it's very warm, isn't it?"

Kate was looking at the pad in her hand, about to turn away.

But Jack kept her a minute. "Oh, I say! You aren't offended, are you? I wouldn't do that for anything."

"No, of course not." But Kate's negation was made only out of a spirit of reserve and also embarrassment. "No."

"But you are, and I don't wonder. Of course you'd be on your cousin's side. And listen. We are, too. Rose and I and all of us are, always have been. We never could see any sense in all the hubbub. It's just been Grandmother and Grandmother's friends. We all thought Elsie was great stuff when she visited Miss Frazier before—— And we're coming to the party to-night, you bet. Only—at this minute Grandmother is sitting right up there in a window where she can see the court, and it might change her, decide her for some reason not to go to-night. She feels that her going formally and giving in, as it were, publicly, is the thing that's going to turn the trick. It's her show, sort of. If we did it first, now, she might be just as bad as ever again, begin all over again. Do you see?"

"No, I don't see," Kate said in all truth. Jack's explanations shed no light whatsoever. His face had grown steadily redder as he realized that he had simply made a mess of it. "I don't see."

But even as she stood looking at Jack Denton she was smiling at herself mentally, to hear how her voice had taken on the very timbre of Elsie's when she was being her most unpleasantly polite. What a copy cat she was. Still, there was a certain satisfaction in finding herself so successful in a self-made rôle. "All you say is just Greek to me. And I ought to be writing my letter. Good morning."

She turned deliberately and sauntered back to her place in the shade of the orchard. But Jack did not leave the wall. He stayed there watching her, a frown gathering on his brow. When she was seated, with her back against an apple tree trunk and her pad ready on her knee, he called again.

"Oh, I say," he called. "I thought you knew everything about it all, of course. If you don't, it's a shame. I just can't be apologetic enough."

But Kate did not turn to him. "Go away, go away, go away," she said, mentally. "I don't want to hear any more. It's not for you to unravel the mystery. I don't want to know from a stranger. I feel very indignant. Very, very indignant, and I hardly know why."

Kate's silence meant as much to Jack Denton as the thoughts he could not hear. He turned away and strolled toward the house, swinging his racket and looking at the ground dejectedly. Kate was sorry she had been so deliberately rude, but she simply could not call him back. She was too really indignant, and at the same time unable to analyze her indignation. She returned to her letter.

But she found it very difficult to write. There was just too much ever to begin to put on paper, in spite of this being only her third day here! What she must do was simply tell the *facts* and let the rest go. The colour of the facts, all that lay underneath and over them, must wait. The letter that finally developed was a thin affair, perfunctory and empty of interest. Kate had never in her life felt so far from her mother.

The girls and Miss Frazier selected and cut flowers in the garden. They took them in loosely on their arms and tossed them down on a damp sheet spread on the floor just inside the drawing-room doors. Then came the deciding on receptacles and the placing of them. It was all very interesting, and exciting, too, for as the rooms grew in adornment Kate felt the party itself drawing nearer and nearer. Miss Frazier seemed very gay as they worked. She laughed and said whimsical things in a whimsical manner. And her every touch was deft, and the result artistic.

That morning Kate learned more about colour values and proportion than she had ever learned in all her years of school. She had not dreamed that so much *mind* could be used on such an apparently simple occupation as placing a few nasturtiums in a vase!

What a good time they were having! Kate moved about the big drawing-room and hall with almost dancing steps, she was so happy doing her aunt's intelligent bidding and seeing loveliness form before her eyes and under her hand. And Elsie was laughing quite spontaneously at Aunt Katherine's humour and taking as much delight as Kate in the growing beauty of the arrangements.

"Someone to speak to you on the telephone, Miss Frazier." Isadora had come out from the telephone booth under the hall stairs.

"Who is it, please? Always get the name, Isadora."

"Yes, ma'am. I always do when I can. But this gentleman won't give his name. Says it's not necessary. He wants to speak to you on important business, he says."

"Won't give his name! Nonsense! Tell him, then——" But suddenly in the middle of this command Aunt Katherine's expression changed. "Oh, well, I think I know now who it must be. That's all right, Isadora."

Aunt Katherine dropped the yellow roses she was sorting—their wet stems and leaves instantly spreading white spots on to the polished surface of the little table. With a quick step she hurried toward the telephone booth. Kate snatched up the roses and remedied the harm they had done as well as she could with her pocket handkerchief. Then she and Elsie simply stood idly about waiting for the doors of the telephone booth to open and their Chieftain to reappear. For having seen Aunt Katherine work with the flowers they knew themselves incompetent to go ahead alone.

As Kate leaned against the banister, and Elsie smoothed her hair before a little gilt mirror on the wall near the door and secured the shell pins holding it, the front-door bell suddenly rang and Isadora came into the hall to answer it. A postman in livery standing there thrust a pad at her mumbling, "Sign here."

Elsie dropped a shell pin on to the floor and rushed to Isadora. "It's a special delivery," she cried. "For me?"

Yes, it was for Elsie. She almost snatched it out of the postman's hands and scrawled her signature on the pad that Isadora surrendered.

"All right," she said, pushing the pad at the postman and the next instant shutting the door directly in his face. Had she shoved him out? Kate was not at all sure she hadn't.

Then Elsie ran through the hall with the letter hugged up under her chin and up the stairs past Kate. "Tell Aunt Katherine I'll be right back," she called as she went. But she stopped on the first landing to lean over the banister and whisper down, "Don't say anything about my having had a special delivery, will you, Kate?"

"Of course not, if you don't want me to. It's none of my business, is it?"

CHAPTER XIII
"YOU THIEF!"

Kate was dressed and ready for the party half an hour before dinner that night. She stood surveying herself in the long door mirror. Anticipation had brought unusual colour that glowed even through the tan on her cheeks, and the corners of her lips were sharply uptilted.

"The cap is certainly a wonder worker," she reflected. "It is magic; it makes me pretty. That's even better than having a cap to make you invisible, much better!" And when she smiled at this idea the girl in the glass smiled, too, and was fascinatingly pretty. "Oh, if Mother could only see me! She'd hardly believe. If the picture telephone were perfected and Aunt had one I'd spend my last cent to call Mother up."

All this was not so conceited as it sounds; for Kate knew perfectly well that ordinarily she could lay no claim to prettiness, that the charm of the person clothed in crocus-yellow satin in the mirror before her was due to Madame Pearl's artistic genius and the pert, star-pointed silver cap. And when the idea came to her to go down to the kitchen and display herself to Julia in this enchantment it was wholly for Julia's pleasure she intended it; she would be taking herself down in the same impersonal way she would take a doll down to turn it round. For finery of this sort and the kind of glamour that beautiful clothes give, she did not for a minute associate with herself, her *very* self. Ever since Julia had appeared to her on the stairs, asked eager questions about her mother and bestowed the gingerbread man on Kate, she had wanted to see her again. It seemed so queer and unnatural to be eating the delicious meals she cooked and ignoring her presence in the house. Wasn't she a friend of her mother's? But until this minute Kate had been too shy or too strange in the ways of her aunt's big smoothly running establishment to seek Julia out in the dim, distant servants' apartments. Now, however, in her magic cap, looking and feeling like a young princess, and also disguised in a way, she had no hesitation about it. She felt sure that Julia would be interested and pleased, and that Katherine, if she were in Kate's place, would do that very thing. But on second thought she decided to wait until just after dinner, for this hour would surely be about the busiest one in a cook's day.

She crossed the room and sat down at her dressing table again, pulling out a drawer. She would reread a letter from Sam, a scrawl that had come in the afternoon's mail when she was too much occupied to give it her full attention. She had merely glanced it down hastily and put it away in this drawer on top of the key to the orchard house. She read it now, bending her head and not bothering to pick it up.

"Don't let her befool you, Kitty. Take our word, she's just a silly snob. You're worth millions of her any minute. What a figure she'd cut in that meadow—you know, with the King of the Fairies! She just wouldn't be *anything*, would she? Teach her a lesson. We'd like to, Lee and I." There was more of the same sort; but she did not pick it up to turn the page. There was an uneasy stirring in her heart. It hadn't been very decent of her, writing like that about Elsie. She could not remember now just how she had done it, or why. She knew that both Sam and Lee must have struggled together over the composition of this letter in reply. They had evidently thought it a very important letter indeed, and spent their best efforts on it. She appreciated that, and she appreciated their hot partisanship, too. What she didn't appreciate at this minute was her own motives in having so called out their sympathy. And she had better tear it up. It certainly wasn't a letter meant for other eyes to see. With a strange little ache in her soul somewhere, probably in her conscience, she picked up the sheet. Then her heart stood still, and the fingers crumpling the paper turned cold. She went queerly sick. The key that should have lain there under the letter was gone. It was nowhere in the drawer. And whoever had taken the key could scarcely have failed to read the words staring there so blackly up at you, all in Sam's print-like script!

Moreover—she saw it now—the thief had gone through the whole dressing table before hitting upon this particular drawer. Everything was a little out of place. The thief was Elsie, of course. No one else wanted the key. Well, serve her right, then, to have read about herself!

Kate tore the letter into shreds and dropped it back into the drawer. Then she strode through the bathroom, and stood in Elsie's open door. Elsie was already decked in her fairy green frock, her curls tied loosely at her neck in a way that Madame Pearl had begged her to wear them. But quite regardless of her finery she was curled up in the window seat, her sandaled feet tucked under her, looking dreamily out toward the orchard house. She was lost in her thoughts for she did not hear or feel Kate when she came striding across the room to stand over her. Even in the temper she was in, Kate could not help thinking, "How unconcerned she is about that beautiful frock! It's as though she was born in it. How delicate, how *fairy* she looks!"

Elsie started out of her reverie at Kate's voice.

"Give me my key," she was saying huskily, her hand held out.

Elsie, in spite of the suddenness of the attack, did not stir except to turn her head.

"What key?"

"You know very well what key. You stole it."

Red scorched Elsie's cheeks at the word "stole." Kate rejoiced at that. She would make it scorch even redder. "You are no better than a thief, to hunt through my things, to read my letters. To steal, to steal, to steal!"

Even as Kate stormed she knew, deep where knowing still had a foothold below the surface of her anger, that her greatest fury was at herself—fury that there had been such a letter for Elsie to read at all, that she had ever written the Hart boys as she had written them. But in spite of that knowing she seemed to have no control over the superficial Kate, the raging, furious Kate.

"You thief! You're no better than a thief! Give me back my key."

But Elsie's response to this attack surprised Kate into a little calmness. She stood up, clenching her hands, and facing her accuser.

"Well, if I am a thief I am proud of it, proud, proud. So there! If you think I'm ashamed of it you're wrong! Call me thief all you like. I like to be called thief. I like it. I am one. I've got your old key. I'll give it to you to-night when we come up to bed, not before. I meant to all along. Then the orchard house will be yours, all yours. Go live in it! I won't care. There's the gong."

But in spite of Kate's growth in calmness her determination remained. "Aunt Katherine gave the key to me," she said. "It belongs to me. Give it back this instant."

"If I won't, what will you do?"

Kate considered. "If you won't, I'll go right out there after dinner and climb in at a window and explore the whole house. I'll discover your blessed secret whatever it is and not even wait till morning. That's what I'll do."

Elsie stood looking at her. But something changed in her eyes. For a flash, or was it only Kate's wild imagining, a comrade looked out through those clouded windows, making them in that instant clear as day, and then vanished. *Now Kate knew what would have been the expression on the face of the fairy in the wood that June day, eight years ago, if she had not flashed back into the sunlight too quickly for her to catch it. It would have been this sky-clear look of the golden comrade.*

"Why don't you say you'll tell Aunt Katherine?"

Kate looked at Elsie, amazed. Such an idea had never entered her head. Her face said so. *Again the comrade flashed.* But it vanished quicker than before, and this time definitely. "Well, you told your wonderful friends, 'The boys,' on me. You *do* tell, you see."

Kate had no answer to that.

Elsie whirled about and went to her bed. From under her pillow she took the key, and returning, handed it to Kate, coolly. "Here it is," she said, "and this is the last time I shall ever ask a favour of you, Kate Marshall. Please don't use it to-night."

Kate accepted the key. "All right," she promised. "I won't use it to-night. There won't be time, anyway, with the party and everything." She was not speaking to the Elsie who had asked the favour, however, but to the vanishing comrade, invisible now, whom she had seen clear enough in that one flash. Was that comrade within hearing, she wondered.

"Thanks," Elsie said, as though she meant it, and in a relieved tone. Then she straightened. "But just the same, Kate Marshall, I shall never, never, never, never forgive you for calling me a thief, not so long as I live, I sha'n't."

"You said you were proud of it," Kate rather cruelly retorted.

Elsie suddenly threw her arm across her eyes. To Kate's dismay she was sobbing.

"Don't cry, don't cry," she begged. "The gong rang minutes ago. Quick, wash your eyes. For Aunt Katherine's sake! She's been so good to us. Let's go on pretending everything's all right."

Masterfully, but very wretched in her heart because of this bitter weeping of which she was the cause, Kate hurried Elsie into the bathroom, ran some cold water into the bowl, and put a wash cloth into her hands. "Quick, wash your eyes. For Aunt Katherine's sake!" Kate commanded again, and Elsie obeyed.

Then Kate took her hand and hurried with her out through the twisted passageways to the main front hall and down the stairs. Dinner had been announced some time ago, and Aunt Katherine was waiting, standing and impatient, in the drawing-room. But when she saw them hurrying and hand-in-hand she smiled. When you have dressed for your first real party in your first real party frock you may be expected to be a little late!

"How lovely you are, Aunt Katherine." Elsie gave her tribute spontaneously in as cool a way as though the scene upstairs had never taken place; and Kate echoed "Lovely, Aunt Katherine."

Miss Frazier was touched. "Thank you, my dears," she said. "And I can return the compliment. In fact, Madame Pearl has outdone herself!"

Miss Frazier deserved their tribute. She was both handsome and distinguished looking, with her graying hair done high and topped with a jewelled comb that sent out shivers of light whenever she moved, gowned in softest lilac-coloured silk draped with black lace, and wearing a long black lace scarf in a most regal manner. The lilac, the green, and the crocus-yellow figures that passed into the dining-room arm-in-arm caused the waitress Effie the most wide-eyed admiration.

"And they were as friendly, just as friendly as could be," she told the kitchen when she removed the service plates. "You'd think Miss Frazier was their mother, she's that affectionate. Why, it's like a regular family to-night!"

Julia, handing out hot dishes, beamed. "Perhaps everything's coming right, after all," she said. "Katherine's child will shed sunshine all about just as Katherine did."

Bertha, sitting at a distant table playing cards with Timothy and the gardener, sniffed at that. "Miss Elsie is as capable of shedding sunshine as anybody," she said, defensively. "She's just made of it herself. I'm always telling you."

"Yes, you're always telling. But we're never seeing," Julia retorted. "Touched with melancholy, she seems to me, but as nice as you please. Only not cheerful to have about. It's probably her poor mother's awful death. Her heart's broke."

Bertha shook her head. "I don't think her heart's broken. She's as gay as anything alone with me sometimes! And she's the most generous child living."

"She does funny things, though," Timothy offered his bit. "Carrying groceries up to her room, buying eggs and bread and stuff and paying for 'em herself. Holt told me."

Bertha looked at him, unbelieving. "Groceries in her room? No such thing. Who takes care of her room, do you think? I never saw such a thing in it. What do you mean?"

Then Timothy related how for a week past Elsie had bought foodstuffs every time she went to the village, and refused to give them to him to carry around to the kitchen afterward. Julia had assured him they were never ordered by her; so of course Miss Elsie took them to her room. Where else could she keep them?

Bertha would have nothing to do with that idea. Indeed, it was impossible there could be any such food supply as Timothy described in Elsie's room, for Bertha knew every inch of that dainty apartment, and kept it in order. Still, she had respect for Timothy, and could not doubt his word when he insisted that Elsie actually had bought bread and eggs, lettuce, oil, and nuts and brought them home with her in the car. "What she does with 'em's none of our business, that I can see," she volunteered. "Feeds the birds in the gardens and orchard perhaps. She's that unselfish! She's probably even kinder to the birds than to human beings."

But every one laughed at this explanation. You don't feed birds eggs and oil and nuts! No, there was some mystery about it. Julia had felt mystery in the air for a week past, and not just because of Elsie's queer purchases and the puzzle of what became of them, either. Mystery was simply "in the air." Julia "*felt*" it.

Timothy nodded his head knowingly. Timothy was Irish and very romantic. "What can you expect?" he asked. "In a house with two young things like that! Why, they've just come out of the Fairyland of their childhood, they're standing now on the edges of life. What can you expect but mystery? They're all mystery."

"I don't mean that kind of mystery, Timothy," Julia protested. "I mean regular down-and-out *mystery*. I feel it in my bones. You wait and see if I'm not right."

Effie had returned from the dining-room again. "Miss Frazier's telling them about Rome now," she said. "She says she'll take them both there together sometime, if Miss Kate's mother'll let her go. She said 'Katherine' just as easy as though it didn't hurt a bit and as though it might be any name. Perhaps she wouldn't mind our speaking it now. Things are changing."

It was true. Things were changing with Miss Frazier. She sat at the head of her table to-night a light-hearted, spirited person. And she was more than that. She was intensely interesting. She said she meant soon to begin to travel, really to travel and see the world. Arabia attracted her, and all Asia. A book by a man named Ferdinand Ossendowski had lately stimulated her roving instincts and enthralled her imagination. Why should she not explore a totally different civilization from the one she had been born into! She recounted some of Ossendowski's exploits, adventures, and escapes, and his stories of the "King of the World." As she talked a panorama entirely new to her listeners unrolled before their minds' visions. What a place this world was, what a place to be alive in, and what a time to be alive! How the importance of personal affairs evaporated in the face of such contemplation! The girls were as stirred as Miss Frazier herself apparently had been stirred; they were lifted out of themselves. They felt that the world was a challenge, that life was a challenge—a glorious one. For the time the party, drawing so near now, sank into insignificance.

But Miss Frazier, looking at their eager faces, suddenly remembered. She said, "Katherine wouldn't let me take you to such out-of-the-way places yet, Kate, and of course I wouldn't want to. But when we go to Rome——" Then she had talked about Rome and places nearer home. But in speaking of them she touched them with a new light and interest. Kate's dream, as most girls' dreams, had often been of some day going "abroad." Such an adventure in contemplation had always seemed the very height of happiness to her. But now, Miss Frazier's conversation lent travel new glamour, for Miss Frazier was steeped in history, the history of nations and religions and art, and her idea of travel was not simply of adventure into lands, but into realms of imagination, and into the past.

"Would you girls like to travel with me for a summer—perhaps next summer?" she asked.

Kate's joy at such a prospect was too great to allow of words. She simply glowed at Aunt Katherine. But Elsie suddenly turned away her head. Somehow then, in that instant, the spell was broken. The dinner table with the diners floated back to Miss Frazier's house in Oakdale, Massachusetts, and there they sat, consuming "cottage pudding" with lemon sauce, dressed and ready for a party.

After dinner Miss Frazier settled down, expecting to finish "The King of the Fairies" before the guests began to arrive, leaving the girls to amuse themselves in their own way. Elsie wandered out on to the star-lighted terrace, looking exactly like a dreamy fairy. Kate went with her, not speaking, and soon leaving her, to find her way around to the kitchen door.

The servants in their own attractive dining-room were just beginning dinner. Kate had forgotten how many of them there would be, and was almost overcome with embarrassment, when they all leapt to their feet and the maids walked around her in a circle, exclaiming admiringly. "I just wanted to show Julia the new frock Aunt Katherine gave me," Kate was explaining a little breathlessly. "I never seem to see you, Julia," she added, catching her eye at last in the group, "and I never really thanked you for the gingerbread man and your kind inquiries about Mother."

"To think," exclaimed Julia, "of my giving you a gingerbread man! Where were my wits? Why, you're a young lady. But your mother liked gingerbread even after she was a young lady."

"You'll have a fine time at your party in that gown," Isadora affirmed. "You couldn't help it. There'll be nothing half so beautiful."

Meanwhile Bertha beamed. In a way she felt responsible for this young vision of splendour. Hadn't she helped choose the dress, and hadn't she finally put Kate into it! She was certainly involved in the display.

Then Julia said, feelingly, "We're all grateful to you, Miss Kate, for bringing a party to this house again, for getting things natural. Miss Frazier's acting like herself now, and it's on account of you."

"Why, I haven't done anything," Kate denied.

But she liked their praise and their warmth, and she felt now entirely in the mood for the party to begin.

CHAPTER XIV
THE STRANGER IN THE GARDEN

Soon after eight Miss Frazier stood regally in the wide hall between her two nieces, receiving and introducing the first arrivals. They came fluttering in at the big wide-open door—girls in shimmering, fluffy party frocks of rainbow colours; boys, mostly in white flannels and dark coats, but a few in tuxedos; and a thin scattering of two older generations, these latter gray-haired grandmothers and younger matrons—some of the mothers looking scarcely older than their own children, in the modern manner. All was murmuring, laughter. Then the orchestra placed back in the blue breakfast-room began tuning their instruments. Jack Denton claimed Kate for the first dance. He danced perfectly, much better than Kate, in fact, who had had little experience; and all the time he kept up a stream of interesting nonsense. Kate laughed at him and swung along more and more in harmony with the music. How gay, how merry it all was! Elsie floated past, her green chiffon draperies like airy wings.

"Isn't she lovely!" Kate exclaimed in admiration that must find voice. "Do you know I think she is the very prettiest——" She was going to say, "the very prettiest girl I have ever seen," but Jack interrupted, his brown eyes smiling down at her: "No, I wouldn't say she's the *prettiest*——"

No one in all her life had ever even insinuated that Kate was pretty before, and the comparison that Jack indicated now was beyond contemplating. It was the magic silver cap, of course. Suppose it should blow off as they danced! How surprised Jack Denton would be!

As the evening went on Kate entertained more and more the conceit that she was masquerading in prettiness. There was no blinking the fact that she was tremendously popular. And it obviously was not just the easy popularity of the girl for whom the party is given. Not a bit of it. It was spontaneous, joyous. Perhaps she realized the reality of this popularity all the more because she had never experienced it before. At the two or three high-school dances in Middletown which her mother had allowed her to attend, while not being exactly a wallflower, she had not particularly shone. There had been many minutes of suspense when she forced a semblance of a smile to her lips and intense interest to her eyes while she watched the more popular girls swinging by with their partners, while all her mind was taken up with praying that Jim Walker or Cecil Quinn would look in from the hall and notice there was a girl there not dancing. It is true that Jim or Cecil or some other usually did notice sometime before the dance was half over and come to her rescue, for Kate was a good sort and everybody liked her. At those dances Kate never counted on the Hart boys for attention, although they were her escorts to and from; for to them Kate was no better than a sister. They would have been glad to see her popular, and taken natural pride to themselves in it. But it never entered their heads to be gallant themselves. No, the high-school dances had left Kate secure in the conviction that she would never be a success socially and in the philosophical determination not to care.

But to-night all that was changed. Even Elsie, perfectly beautiful as she was, was not having the same success. She danced constantly, of course, but often with a boy whom Kate had had to refuse.

In an intermission a dowager-like old lady beckoned to Kate from a chair near an open door leading out on to the terrace. Kate left Jack Denton who at the minute was fanning her with a magazine which he had picked up from a table for the purpose, and went to the dowager.

"Bring a chair," the bejewelled one commanded, "and talk to an old woman for a minute."

And when Kate had drawn up a stool that stood near and sat down close to her she said, "You are every bit as pretty as your mother was, Katherine Marshall. Every bit!"

Kate shook her head, laughing. "It's just a disguise," she affirmed, mysteriously.

"A disguise? What do you mean, you funny child?"

"This cap I am wearing is a magic cap," Kate informed her, touching its star points ever so lightly with her finger tips. "But shh! don't let them hear. I will confess to you, though, that it makes me much, much better looking than I really am, and more popular."

The evening had rather gone to Kate's head. But the dowager person liked it. She liked it very much. She tapped Kate's shoulder with her jewelled lorgnette. "Well, then, shall I say," she continued quite in Kate's fantastic mood, "you have your mother's prettiness to begin with, and on top of that the magic cap has added a good bit more. But even better than prettiness you have her spirit. She was always the belle of every party. And often I've sat right here in this very chair and watched her gliding past with the young men. Dancers did glide then, not hop and walk. In spite of her preoccupation she always gave me a smile as she drifted. And I was old and ugly even then."

"Old and ugly! Are you wearing a magic something yourself to-night, then? Perhaps it's your pearls that make you seem stately and lovely!"

There was blarney in this, for while the dowager was stately enough she certainly was not lovely in any usual sense of the word.

But Kate was scarcely responsible. She hardly knew what she was saying; she was simply effervescing with high spirits and a heady self-satisfaction.

The dowager laughed mellowly. She was not often mellow, and certainly she had not been mellow before this evening. She had sat perfectly still in her chair, her hands folded, with the expression of a judge in court. Now, however, she was a judge no longer. She had slipped into the spirit of the party, swept in on Kate's fantasy. Miss Frazier watching, but not appearing to watch, from a distant divan where she conversed with two or three mothers, saw the mellowing even at that distance and was well pleased. "Congratulations, Kate," she said, mentally. "Congratulations, and thank you."

Meanwhile the dowager was murmuring in Kate's ear: "You are a dear! It's for your mother's and your grandfather's sake I came to-night and persuaded my daughter to let the young people come. And now I am glad I did."

Kate looked up at her. "Why for their sake? Why not come, anyway?" But as she spoke automatically, Kate felt her lips stiffening over the words. Indignation was suddenly welling up as it had in the garden with Jack Denton that morning. Glamour fled away, and Kate was straightening like a warrior.

But the dowager hardly heard her question, and certainly did not notice the straightening process. She went on, "I always said no good would come of it. There's something in good blood that tells—and in bad blood, too. Not that we knew the blood was bad—although in time it showed it was surely enough—just that we didn't know anything about it! How Miss Frazier dared, a person of her race and blood——"

But Kate interrupted with a strained laugh. "Blood!" she wanted to exclaim. "You make me creep. Are you Lady Macbeth's grandmother?" But she uttered no sound except the laugh. This was fortunate for Kate, and remarkable restraint. She sat with lips stiffened, watching the glamour gliding away out of her heart, out of the party.

The dowager had paused a minute at Kate's laugh, waiting for her to speak. But now she continued, "Terrible risk. Everyone warned her. But she would listen to nobody, not even to me. Now she's trying to unmake her bed. It's to be hoped she sees the folly of expecting anything good to be made out of bad blood. Environment! Pshaw! Futile!"

Kate shivered. She looked around for a way of escape from this murmuring, croaking person whom but a minute ago she had dubbed stately and lovely. If she should start now and dance off on the music that was beginning again might she outdance the spectre? Might she overtake the glamour? There was Elsie, standing alone for the minute in the open doorway a few steps away. Kate knew now why she had outdistanced Elsie in popularity to-night; she knew it as she watched her, hardly aware of thinking about it at all. Elsie was too fine, too entirely lovely in the real meaning of the word to appeal to any but those sensitive to loveliness in its purest essence. She did not belong to the party at all. She belonged to the starlight beyond the lamplight, to the dim orchard—to the orchard house!

"Whom will you dance this with?" the dowager was inquiring in Kate's ear.

"The first person that gets here," Kate replied, quickly. But the dowager did not take offence. Several were in the race, but a tall, lanky youth won, a humorous creature with a happy-go-lucky bearing. When Kate rose to dance off with him, the dowager took her hand. She smiled up at her in the most friendly manner. "You must come to call on me soon," she said. "Or I will call for you and take you for a drive and then home for tea. That will be better, I think. How is that?"

"Thank you." Kate managed to smile, but it was a smile her mother would never have recognized.

"I'll say," her partner informed her the minute they were out of hearing, "you've made a hit. Do you know who she is? Jack Denton's grandmother, Mrs. Van Vorst-Smith. The social autocrat of Oakdale. Everything will come your way now."

But Kate did not respond to this gay assurance. "What's the matter?" her partner asked, surprised. Responsiveness had been Kate's greatest charm all the evening, if she had only known it, not the cap.

"Nothing. Only I'm chilly."

The boy whistled. "No wonder, having sat next to that old iceberg so long. Though 'twas probably the air from the door, too. It's lots cooler and a storm is coming up, I think. I'd have rescued you sooner if I'd had the nerve. She looked almost outlandishly amiable, though. What was her line?"

Kate shivered, a pretend shiver this time, getting her gaiety back. "Blood! Just blood, if you will believe me. Is she an ogress as well as a social autocrat? She discussed blood in several of its phases. Bad blood, good blood, and talking blood. Like the singing bone, I suppose."

The boy laughed heartily. "She didn't waste any time in mounting her hobby, I'll say. But she can't worry you. Your blood's all right. That's the word's been going 'round ever since the invitations were out. 'Fraziers, one of the best families in Massachusetts.' She was probably congratulating you and expecting a return of the compliment."

Kate laughed. But in spite of her new gaiety, the corners of her mouth had quite lost their winged tilt.

After a few more dances, supper was announced. Kate had promised Jack Denton early in the evening that she would take supper with him. She saw him now looking about for her. In an instant their eyes would meet and he would hurry across to her where she stood for the minute alone. But she suddenly realized that she was tired. She ached with too much dancing. She would never have acknowledged this to herself, of course, unless something had gone wrong with the evening. Hardly knowing why, she stepped out of the door near which she was for the instant standing, backward. That step precipitated her into a different world entirely. The stars had disappeared behind dark, windy rain clouds. The air was fresh, and you heard a wind and felt its edges. Kate took a deep breath. She would stay here in the blowy dark just for a little. It wouldn't hurt Jack to search a minute longer.

She moved, still backward, farther away from the lighted doorway. She brushed against a garden chair and sat down. She leaned her head against its high back. An impulse came to take off the magic silver cap and be herself. Whimsically she lifted it from her head and placed it on her knee.

"Now you're just Kate Marshall," she spoke to herself, but aloud. "Just ordinary, plain-as-day Kate Marshall. Dowagers can't spoil anything for you. They wouldn't pay enough attention to you now to bother about spoiling. All the magic that's really your own, all that isn't false magic, she can't touch. Nothing she could say could touch it."

Kate sighed, having finished her little heartfelt speech to herself. She felt relieved and freshened. She had certainly cast off the dowager's spell.

"That's right. All the magic that's your own, nobody, even a Mrs. Van Vorst-Smith, can touch. It's safer than the stars from troubling!"

That was a low voice speaking directly behind her. No, it was not simply her own thoughts, although those words might very well have been in her mind that minute, for some of them were right out of "The King of the Fairies." But it had been a voice, a man's voice.

Slowly she turned her head. Directly behind her chair a man was standing. She could not see his features at all, because the night was so black, but she thought that he was hatless, and she knew he was in dark clothes. The wind, not merely its edges, had come to earth now. Was it flapping the borders of a long dark cape enveloping the vague figure?

The vague figure bent down to her. Yes, it was a dark cape, blowing away from his shoulders on the wind. It seemed as though the being himself leaned down out of the wind. "Give this to Elsie, please," he said, in quite a matter-of-fact tone now. Then the wind took him. At least Kate could not see him any more. He had stepped back among the tall lilac bushes that bordered the terrace at that spot.

When he was gone it was just exactly as though he had never been, except for the folded paper that Kate found clutched in her hand. That folded paper, however, definitely fixed him as a reality. But who could it have been? Mr. O'Brien, the detective, crossed Kate's mind, or one of his assistants, that young man of the polka-dotted tie. But instantly she laughed, though silently, at such a notion. They, neither of them, she felt sure, would by any chance have quoted from "The King of the Fairies" while doing business. "It's safer than the stars from troubling." Had the King of the Fairies himself passed her there on the wind? No, hardly. He wouldn't be leaving a note for Elsie.

Anyway, whoever it might be, he had spoken in a voice whose bidding she was ready to follow. She rose and took the few steps between the chair and the drawing-room door. But she stepped over the sill without hurry, with a meditative air. The man, standing a little way in among the tall lilac bushes, said to himself; "She's the right stuff. Not startled or upset. Good for Kate Marshall!"

Jack Denton pounced upon her almost at once. "Where *have* you been?" he cried. "The salad I fought for and won for you has just been commandeered by my grandmother. Now will you agree to stay put while I dash into the fray in the dining-room again?"

"Yes, after a minute. First I must find Elsie. I have to see her very specially."

"Elsie? Haven't laid eyes on her for some time. Give me your message and I'll go hunt."

"No, but do look around for her. I will, too, and that will save time."

Elsie was not to be found anywhere in all the rooms that were lighted and open that evening on the first floor of the house. "She's just not down here at all, unless she's somewhere in the servants' wing," Jack finally reported when they met by chance at the foot of the stairs.

Kate now went to her aunt who was having salad sitting between two dowagers, one of them Kate's dowager. "I am looking for Elsie, Aunt Katherine," she said. "Have you seen her recently?"

Miss Frazier shook her head. "Not for some time. I myself have been wondering what has become of her." Miss Frazier's dark eyes as she lifted them to Kate were clouded with worried surmise.

Mrs. Van Vorst-Smith laughed. As a laugh, it sounded a trifle unsure of itself and uneasy for a dowager person. "I had a few words with the child myself half an hour or so ago," she volunteered. "Strangely enough, she took some offence at some remarks that were meant only kindly, and flounced off. Perhaps she is sulking somewhere about it."

"I am sorry, Mrs. Van Vorst-Smith, if my niece was rude to you." But in spite of the words Miss Frazier's tone was not at all a sorry tone; it was rather edged. She herself had just been submitted to some remarks of Mrs. Van Vorst-Smith's that were doubtless meant kindly, and as a consequence her sympathy was all with Elsie. But even so, if Elsie were sulking, she was undoing all that Miss Frazier's efforts had built up in her behalf. That was a pity.

"Don't apologize for the young person you call your niece," Mrs. Van Vorst-Smith said, suavely. "We will lay it simply at the door of the times. There is no respect for age, say nothing of *birth*, in this generation."

Miss Frazier paid slight attention to these acid remarks. She merely said to Kate in a concerned tone, "I'd go upstairs to look for her, Kate. Under no circumstances must the party be ruined for her by *anybody*. Do persuade her to come back and forget any hurts she may have received. Do your best."

Kate flew away on the errand, her heart rejoiced that her aunt had answered the dowager exactly as she had.

There was no light in the girls' suite. "She can't be here," Kate decided. But just to make absolutely certain she went through and, fumbling for it, turned on the switch just inside Elsie's door.

The first thing that caught her eye under the shaded lights that blossomed forth so obediently at the pressure of her finger was the fairy green frock dropped in a heap exactly in the middle of the floor, the white sandals topping it! Elsie herself was undressed and in bed!

"Go away, go away," she commanded, plaintively, not even looking to see who was in the room.

Kate stood dumbfounded. Then she remembered her aunt's clouded, kind eyes, and the dowager's haughty, skeptical nose. She braced herself. "I can't go away," she said softly, evenly. "Not until you get up and get dressed and come downstairs with me. How can you treat Aunt Katherine so?"

"I won't get dressed. I won't go down again. I hate the party! It's your party, anyway. I'm not needed down there."

Was Aunt Katherine right in the theory she had put forward at the Green Shutter Tea Room? Was Elsie simply jealous? But Kate rejected that thought almost before it had presented itself. In fact, she caught only the tail of it as it switched by! She spoke reasonably.

"Yes, it's my party so-called. But you know perfectly well that Aunt Katherine means it even more for you. It's so that you'll get to be friendly with all the girls and boys who you say hardly speak to you. My being here was just an opportunity. Now if you vanish in the very middle of things, how do you think that will help any of us? It will be just unspeakable."

"I want to be unspeakable. Go away."

"Yes, perhaps you do. You are, anyway. But do you want Aunt Katherine to be ashamed? Could you ever forgive yourself for treating her so? She knows Mrs. Van Vorst-Smith has been rude to you, and she herself just now has come very near being rude to Mrs. Van Vorst-Smith on your account. Whatever all the fuss is about—honestly and truly I haven't an idea what it is about myself—Aunt Katherine is all for you, Elsie. She's your champion. You can't go back on her now, right before everyone. It doesn't matter whether you're having a good time, not a bit. If you're any good at all you'll get dressed in a jiffy and go back down with me. You can *pretend* you're having a good time."

Kate finished. Her argument had exhausted her strangely. She found herself trembling with the intenseness of her conviction that Aunt Katherine must be saved from all embarrassment.

For a few minutes Elsie made no visible response to the harangue but lay perfectly still, her eyes shut, her head turned away. Kate stood in the middle of the room, the fairy green dress at her feet, waiting. "I've done all I can," she told herself. "Now we'll just see whether she has any sense at all."

After a space of utter stillness Elsie stirred, threw back the coverlet, and sat up. "You're right, I suppose," she said, sulkily. "I'm just a pig, that's all. I was only thinking of myself."

She did not look at Kate but busied herself picking up her scattered clothes. When Kate started to leave the room, however, she called her back. "Do you mind helping me with these?" she asked almost humbly. "I don't want to ring for Bertha. Do you mind?"

"Of course not. Let's hurry. Everybody'll be wondering."

But now when Kate's hands were needed she was recalled to the note still clutched in her fingers.

"Oh, I entirely forgot," she exclaimed, dismayed. "Here is a note for you."

Elsie unfolded the paper. If she had looked miserable before, when she had finished reading the few words on that paper she looked tragic. "Who gave it to you? How did you get it?"

Kate was amazed at the way petulance had turned to sorrow.

"I don't know who, or even exactly how," she confessed. "I was alone for a second on the terrace. A man appeared just out of the wind in a blowing, long cape. He had a singing voice at first so I hardly knew whether he was real. And he quoted 'The King of the Fairies.'"

Elsie nodded. Nothing in Kate's account surprised her apparently. The girls did not speak to each other again but silently worked together repairing the damage done to Elsie's hair-dressing, getting her into the fairy green dress, and finally bathing away evidences of tears. Supper was just about over downstairs before they were ready to descend, and dance strains sounding. Jack had not given Kate up, however, but was faithfully waiting for her on the stairs.

He saw the girls the minute they appeared at the upper turning, and bounded up several steps to meet them. "Where have you been hiding?" he asked, laughingly, and without any signs of surprise whatever. "I've managed to save some salad for you both and ices, too, here in the window seat."

It was a window seat on the stairs, halfway down the first flight. "Oh, thanks," Kate said, heartily. "Have you had some yourself, though?"

"Hardly likely, not until you came. Didn't you promise to have supper with me?" Jack looked feigned surprise and grief.

He was certainly making their return to society easier. Girls and boys glanced up at them rather curiously as they danced past the drawing-room door, and a few of the mothers, sitting where they had a view of the stairs and the landing, rather stared. But since the truants could laugh and talk with Jack, who was acting as though their absence had been in no way extraordinary, they had no time to be self-conscious.

But suddenly Jack's face went queer right in the middle of some nonsense. It was half a laugh, half dismay that twisted his countenance. Quick as thought, he pointed up to the second turn of the stairs. "That's a fine old clock!" he exclaimed. "Take me up and show it to me."

Why they obeyed his command so docilely—put their plates down again on the window seat and went back up the stairs—they hardly knew. But they did go, like lambs. And when they had turned a corner and were out of sight of dancers and chaperons Jack stopped, not looking at the clock at all, and dropped his eyes to Elsie's feet. Even Elsie laughed when she saw what he was calling attention to. In their hurry the girls had forgotten one item, and here was Elsie ready to appear in the drawing-room in her pink satin, swansdown-edged boudoir slippers. They were very dainty slippers, quite fetching in fact, but they were hardly in harmony with the fairy green frock.

"Run back and change while Kate and I admire the clock," Jack advised. And Elsie ran.

When she returned the three sat on the window seat and ate their long-delayed supper. At first Elsie said she wasn't hungry and couldn't possibly eat, but Jack laughed her out of that. Soon Rose came up to join them, carrying her ice, and stopping to take dainty tastes as she came.

"This is the nicest situation of all," she exclaimed, settling down beside Elsie. "And what a view it offers. Why, it's like being in a box at the theatre. We saw you and Kate, by the way, at 'The Blue Bird.' We thought it very grand of you to have a whole box to yourselves."

Others followed Rose, some of them with plates of ice cream. And Kate noticed that the ices and the ice cream were in every case in a stage of melting. She suspected then that Jack had overheard the conversation about the missing Elsie and had collected this little band, encouraging them to *eat slowly*. The realization of his tact and consideration wiped out for ever any lurking indignation toward him left over from the morning, when he had squirmed at the idea of her calling Elsie down to play tennis.

A few minutes later, when Miss Frazier came out into the hall with old Mrs. Van Vorst-Smith who was leaving and seemed to require her escort, she saw to her great surprise and relief that the very merriest part of the party was on the stairs. There were eight or nine girls and boys crowded about Kate and Elsie talking eagerly and interrupting themselves with the lightest-hearted laughter. No need to worry any more now because her girls were not on the floor dancing. This was an even better way of getting acquainted. Mrs. Van Vorst-Smith, feeling for an instant that she had lost the full attention of her hostess, followed her gaze upward. Kate was looking down, and their eyes met. Then old Mrs. Van Vorst-Smith did an amazing thing. At least, the few people who observed it were amazed. She made the motion of "good-night" with her lips to Kate, and *blew her a kiss*.

Both her grandchildren stared round-eyed. "I say," Jack whispered, "you have certainly charmed my grandmother. What did you ever do to her?"

He looked at Kate, wonderingly respectful, with frankest curiosity.

When Miss Frazier returned from seeing the old lady out of the door, she stood for a minute within hearing of the conversation on the stairs. They were discussing "The Blue Bird" now, but presently it changed to "The King of the Fairies," a book they all had read, apparently. She smiled inwardly, well pleased. "Katherine over again," she told herself. But she had to admit, too, that Elsie was doing her share in keeping the subject at a high-water-mark of intelligent conversation. "Kate is certainly having an influence," she reflected, "an even finer influence than I could have hoped for." Then she passed on into the drawing-room, trailing her black scarf more regally than ever since she was so honestly proud of both her nieces.

When the last guest had departed Miss Frazier took an arm of each niece and led them toward the stairs. "It was all a great success," she affirmed. "And it was you girls, yourselves, who made it a success. Kate, you were what a new girl—at least, any new girl worth her salt—ought to be, the belle of the ball. And, Elsie, you did me more than credit. I am, oh, so very proud of both my girls. Old maiden aunt that I am, I felt that I had two lovely daughters. Now I advise you to dash to bed and save all discussion of the party until morning. Breakfast is ordered for half-past nine to-morrow, so that you may sleep."

"But sha'n't we help you close up?" Elsie offered. "I heard you tell Isadora to go to bed."

"No, thank you, my dear. I am going to stay down here awhile, finishing 'The King of the Fairies.' I was almost at the last chapter when Mrs. Van Vorst-Smith led the procession of arrivals. It is an enchanting story, just as you said. Now, good-night."

For all its finality the "good-night" was spoken with greatest affection. In the last few hours Aunt Katherine had flowered into a serenely warm human being. Both Kate and Elsie realized the change in her, and each, for a different reason, was disturbed by it; Kate because now less than ever she understood how her mother ever could have let such a lovely person go out of her life; and Elsie—well, that concerns the secret of the orchard house.

CHAPTER XV
KATE ON GUARD

Kate was waked by the flapping of her window draperies. The rain that had held off during the evening was upon them now, a wild, windy, heavy rain, unusual for July. Kate heard it spattering on the floor of the balcony and pattering on the floor inside the tall windows. This last would never do. Much as she liked the fresh wet wind, full of garden and damp earth smells, she must close those windows or the room would be damaged. It was pitchy dark, and Kate could be guided only by sound and the direction from which the wind blew. Somehow she got the big door windows closed and fastened, simply by the sense of touch, and then turned gratefully bedward. But she did not go back to bed that night.

Elsie's door had blown shut to only a crack, and light was coming through that crack. That was perhaps none of Kate's business, but instantly she was concerned. She and Elsie had not said "good-night" to each other, but parted in silence. And Kate had gone to sleep wondering just how much Elsie was truly hurt by whatever it was that old Mrs. Van Vorst-Smith had said to her, and wanting, but lacking the courage, to go in and sit on the edge of her bed to talk it out and comfort her if she could. If she had heard Elsie so much as turn in bed she would have taken heart; but not a sound had come from the other room after the light was out. In the end Kate had gone to sleep still undecided as to what she ought to do.

Now the light drew her. Perhaps Elsie had not been to sleep at all. Perhaps she was too unhappy to sleep. Kate had no idea what time it was, and she did not think of the time. Her only anxiety was that Elsie might not be angry with her for trying to comfort. On bare feet she crossed the bathroom floor and pushed at the door.

The lamp by Elsie's bed was burning, but she had placed her party frock over it to dull its glow, so the room was in a queer green light. That was what Kate noticed first. The bed was empty. But Kate found Elsie at once, her back turned to her, and still unconscious of her presence, at the farther end of the room bending over a suitcase which she was busy packing. Elsie was fully dressed, even to her hat. She was wearing the green silk of their Boston jaunt, and the same brown straw hat. It was perfectly plain that she was running away, running away in the middle of a black, stormy night.

Kate pushed the door all the way open. "What are you doing?" she whispered, loudly.

Elsie turned upon her. She had been crying as she packed, and even in the excitement of the moment Kate reflected how oddly tears and a set, tragic face went with the jaunty costume with its brave flutter of orange at the neck.

"You belong in bed," Elsie whispered back. "And any one can see what I'm doing."

"Yes. Running away!"

"Yes, running away. And no business of yours."

The warrior in Kate straightened. This was a clear call to arms. She felt very old and wise. She certainly would never let that crying little girl go away like this into the rain and dark night. She couldn't expect to walk out right under Kate's nose!

"Is that what the note I brought you was about?" she asked. "Was it a plan for this?"

"No. It was telling me *not* to do this. But I'm going to, just the same. He didn't understand—he couldn't know."

Elsie returned to her packing. Kate moved nearer to her.

"Do you think I'm going to stand here and *let* you run away right in the middle of the night like this?" she asked, curiously.

Elsie did not glance up at her. She simply said, "Well, what can you do to stop me?"

"Wake the house, of course. Call Aunt Katherine. Shout for her."

Elsie stared at Kate in unfeigned surprise. "You'd tell on me?" she asked in an unbelieving tone. "I thought you weren't like that. I thought you were decent."

"I am decent. I don't tell, not about little things, like the key. But this is entirely different. I should certainly wake the whole house if you tried to walk out with that suitcase."

"You wouldn't." Elsie lifted the suitcase which was filled and closed now, and picking up her hand-bag from where it lay on the dressing table, took a step toward the door. But Kate reached it ahead of her.

"I'll shout," Kate warned.

"Kate Marshall, please, please, please don't!"

"I certainly will."

Elsie began to cry silently and stood with her suitcase in one hand, her bag in the other, and her face turned from Kate, ashamed of her tears. Kate's heart softened, but not her determination.

"Get undressed and into bed, and promise you won't get out again to-night, or I shall go right to Aunt Katherine's room now and tell her," Kate said firmly.

After a moment of hesitation Elsie began to pull off her clothes furiously. In about two minutes she was in bed, her face turned toward the wall. In silence Kate picked up the cast-off garments Elsie had scattered, and put them away. The green suit she hung up on a hanger in the closet and the hat she put away in the deep hat-drawer. Then the suitcase claimed her attention. Bertha had better not find it packed and standing by the door in the morning. Kate unlatched it and took out the things. "The King of the Fairies" lay at the bottom of them all, with a little New Testament. Kate put the two books on Elsie's bedside table under the lamp. Still Elsie did not move or speak; she might have been asleep for any sign she made that she knew what was occupying Kate in the room.

But Kate spoke to her: "You've burned a hole in your party dress," she said.

It was true. The heat from the electric bulb had been strong enough to scorch the flimsy material.

"No matter," Elsie muttered from her pillow. "I'll never wear it again, anyway."

She had not taken the trouble even to look at the damage. That told Kate, if it still needed telling, how truly desperate Elsie was.

"I'm going into my room," Kate announced, after she had hung the ruined party dress away. "But don't think I'm going to bed, for I'm not. I shall be sitting up, wide awake, and surely hear you if you get up again."

Elsie did not answer.

Kate did not mind that. If never before, now she certainly merited Elsie's wrath. Elsie had hated her before without any cause. There was a certain comfort to Kate in knowing the cause of her present state of mind, a certain satisfaction in no longer being scorned for nothing, but for something. She could defend herself to herself now.

But could she defend herself adequately? Had she really any business to have so interfered with Elsie's plans? Had she any reason so at a leap to have become a dyed-in-the-wool tattletale, at least to have threatened tattletaling? Yes, she thought she could excuse herself. She thought she was more than justified. Even so it was a hateful business.

Kate wrapped herself in her dressing gown and sat in a wicker chair by her reading light. She did not dare lie in bed to think for fear she would drop off to sleep. She gave herself up to pondering the situation, but kept an ear cocked all the while for the slightest movement in the other room.

What should she do about things in the morning? Even if Elsie had failed to get off to-night, if Aunt Katherine were left unwarned, she would certainly plan so as not to fail the next time. Why, to-morrow morning itself Elsie might walk out of the house and never come back. If Elsie had any place to go to, Kate would not be so worried. But she knew that Elsie's mother's family, what there was of it, was living in Europe, and that not one member of it had ever shown the least consciousness of Elsie's existence. Aunt Katherine had told her about that and marvelled at it. So Elsie had just no one to take her in if she did run away. There was the stranger in the garden! But he had told her not to run away. Kate was sure Elsie had spoken truth about that note. Who *was* the stranger in the garden? His note had turned Elsie tragic, whoever he was.

There was no way out of it that Kate could see but telling. Elsie must be protected against herself.

But half an hour's more pondering brought Kate to the conclusion that she would not tell *Aunt Katherine*. Her whole instinct was against that. Aunt Katherine, charming as she was, and kind, was after all only an aunt, and an aunt who had said herself that she simply could not like Elsie. What Elsie needed was a *mother*. This was work for Katherine. Kate had perfect confidence that if her mother could talk with Elsie everything would come clear for everybody. Light suddenly dawned in Kate's puzzled mind. Katherine might take Elsie home with her. They would all three go back to Ashland together, and there all would be made right for Elsie. Once with Katherine's arms around her shoulders, and Katherine's gentle, understanding eyes looking into hers, Elsie would confide. Kate never doubted for an instant that her mother would be overjoyed to take the beautiful, unhappy Elsie to her heart. Why, since Aunt Katherine had failed so to make her happy, and since she did not even like this foster-niece, it might become a permanent arrangement; Elsie would live with them. She would be a sister!

All this was rather wild dreaming. Kate straightened mentally and pulled herself back to hard facts. The facts were simply that Kate could not bring herself to the idea of delivering Elsie up to Aunt Katherine for judgment or help, either one. Elsie needed a mother more than she needed anything else in the world. Katherine was a mother. Katherine must come.

And only a few hours ago Kate had felt very far away from her mother, very independent of her! She smiled now, remembering. Well, she had never needed her more. Sitting alone here in the sleeping house, with rain and wind at the windows and Elsie lying hating her in the next room, Kate *ached* for her mother.

She decided to write her a special delivery letter. That would bring her day after to-morrow, or day after to-day rather, for it must be getting toward day now. For one day Kate could stand guard over Elsie. She was glad of her decision to write as soon as she arrived at it. It seemed automatically to relieve her from grave responsibility. Besides, the composition of the letter would keep her awake.

And so, mother darling, please come on the very first train. Your desperate KATE.

It had been a long, full letter. She had told Katherine just everything that had to do with Elsie and her strange behaviour from their very first meeting. When Kate looked up from her signature she found the night had passed; dawn was in the room, at least the gray light of a rainy morning.

Kate rose, stretched her cramped limbs, and yawned prodigiously. Then she crept to Elsie's door. Elsie was not asleep. Their eyes met. There were dark circles under Elsie's eyes, and her face in the gray light was almost paper-white. The girls stared at each other silently. Then Elsie turned her head away on the pillow.

"How she hates me!" Kate thought, as she stole back through the bathroom. "She's a dreadful hater. I couldn't hate any one that way, no matter what they had done."

She turned out the light that was still burning by her bed. Then she took a cold shower bath and dressed in a fresh dress, the second chintz curtain one. She brushed her hair vigorously.

"Some difference," she reflected, "between the party Kate and the morning-after one. Too bad I haven't a magic cap for day-times!"

Perhaps she needed one especially to-day. For tired, sleepless people are rarely pretty people; and Kate's eyes were almost as dark-rimmed as Elsie's.

Her toilet completed, she stole again to Elsie's door. Again their eyes met.

"If I were you I'd go to sleep," Kate whispered. Elsie's pallor bothered her. But Elsie did not deign to answer.

Kate, back in her room, with over four hours before breakfast stretching away ahead of her, curled up on the foot of the bed with "The King of the

Fairies" in her hands. She opened it just anywhere, much as one opens conversation with a friend just anywhere. It is the *presence* you want. And the presence of the soul in this book did not fail her now. How it drove walls backward and pushed roofs skyward! And as for out-of-doors, it made that boundless, lifting veils and veils of air disclosing Fairyland or Paradise, in any case the realler than real.

Kate was withdrawing from the chintz-curtained Kate on the bed. She was rising up out of that drowsy figure. She was floating. But the flowers from the chintz were still decking her, only they were living flowers now, smelling all the sweeter for the rain soaking their petals. And the birds from the chintz were with her, too, changed to living birds, soaring, floating, drifting with her, singing shrilly in the rain. The mysterious, many-coloured portals of sleep were opening to her far off beyond the last lifted veil of air.

It was nine-fifteen before she woke.

CHAPTER XVI
ONE END OF THE STRING

Breakfast was served in the little blue-and-white breakfast-room. A fire burned there cheerfully in the grate, making it possible to leave the doors open on to the rain-beaten terrace. The storms of the night had subsided into a steady, hard downpour.

"What a day!" Miss Frazier exclaimed when she appeared.

Kate had come into the room just ahead of her. Moved by an impulse of affection she went to her aunt and kissed her on the cheek. "Thank you for that beautiful party," she said. "It was gorgeous."

Miss Frazier was pleased. "Thank you, my dear, for paying back so, in being happy about it, the little that is done for you. 'It is more blessed to give than to receive' may be, but the art of receiving graciously is a rare and beautiful accomplishment. I hope Elsie's experience with Mrs. Van Vorst-Smith didn't entirely keep the evening from being 'gorgeous' for her, too. Where is she?"

"Dressing, I think."

At this moment Miss Frazier was summoned to the telephone. "The same gentleman who wouldn't give his name yesterday," Isadora informed her.

"Don't wait for me, Kate. I'm not having grapefruit."

When Aunt Katherine returned it was plain to see that she was greatly stirred, though trying hard to be calm and matter-of-fact.

"I shall have to go to town," she told Kate. "And I shall be gone all day, probably until rather late to-night. In spite of the rain I think I had better take the car."

Then Elsie came in. She sat down languidly at the breakfast table and leaned her cheek on her hand. Everything that Effie offered she refused.

"Aren't you going to have any breakfast at all?" Miss Frazier asked.

"No. I thought I could eat. But when I see things I know I can't. I think I'll be excused if I may."

Miss Frazier looked at her keenly. "I am afraid you are ill. Come, let me feel your forehead. Yes, it is hot. You have a temperature almost certainly. And the shadows under your eyes! Is this what a party does to you? What a pity that I must leave for Boston at once."

She turned to the maid Effie. "Effie, tell Bertha to get Doctor Hanscom on the telephone and ask him to come over here before office hours. Then she is to help Elsie back to bed."

"Bed! Oh, no. Please! Please, Aunt Katherine!"

"Why, yes. Bed isn't so terrible as all that! You may read or knit, until Doctor Hanscom arrives and gives other orders, anyway. Kate will sit with you so that you won't be lonely. Yes, indeed, you must go to bed."

Elsie was very much distressed at this turn of affairs. Kate saw dismay in her face, and she easily guessed the reason. Of course, being tucked up in bed and getting the attention and care of an invalid would make running away to-day almost impossible. But there was no question of Miss Frazier's being obeyed. She expected obedience and she got it.

When Elsie had left the room Miss Frazier forced herself to take up conversation lightly and naturally for the remainder of the meal, but Kate did not fail to notice that her fingers shook slightly as she lifted her toast and that her dark eyes were unusually bright. Evidently the "gentleman who will not give his name" had had some news of importance. Kate felt confident that that gentleman was the detective, Mr. O'Brien.

"I finished your book last night," Miss Frazier was saying. "I understand your enthusiasm. It is literature and much more. The author must have deep and even esoteric wisdom. One wonders very much who and what he is, the author. But whoever he is, even if this book is all he has to show, he is a great man. Has it occurred to you, Kate, how much, how extraordinarily, like your mother, Hazel, the girl in the story, is? It might be a direct portrait."

Kate laughed. "Oh, have you discovered that, too? Even Mother had to admit it—that in looks, anyway, Hazel was exactly herself when she was that age. But I say she is still like Hazel, old as she is!"

"Thirty-six isn't exactly aged, you know. One might very well keep some remnants of looks even until then." Aunt Katherine was smiling. "But it is a strange coincidence how a person of the imagination can so echo a person in life. I was fairly startled last night when I realized how vivid the resemblance was."

But though Kate heard and replied to all her aunt's remarks during that breakfast, her mind was most of the time on other matters, and if Miss Frazier could have known, Kate under her calm exterior was hiding a heart as perturbed as her own.

Kate was glad when Miss Frazier rose. She assured her that she was very well able to amuse herself at home this rainy day, and that she would do everything for Elsie that she could. Yes, she would see to it that she stayed in bed! Yes, she would read to her, if Elsie felt like listening. Yes, Aunt Katherine was not to worry. And so Miss Frazier departed, and Kate was left virtually in charge of the house, the responsibility for things quite hers.

Of course, Kate knew perfectly well that Elsie would not want her to sit with her, no need even to ask about that. And Kate must hurry to send her telegram. Beyond the portals of sleep she had decided, or possibly it had been decided for her, that the special delivery letter would not make things happen quickly enough. Katherine must be wired for. She was needed to-day. Kate had waked with this determination full-blown. But how could she risk leaving the house now to send the wire, with Elsie in the desperate mood that was so obvious? How could Kate be sure that Bertha would not help Elsie to run away in her absence? Bertha adored Elsie, and Kate herself had reason to know that when Elsie pleaded it was easier to do her wish than not. She realized, of course, that a telegram may be given over the telephone; but her inexperience and shyness made her doubt her ability in such a complicated procedure. Besides, the bill would be charged to Aunt Katherine in that case.

"I shall just have to chance it," she decided. "Elsie needn't know I am out of the house at all, and I can hurry." She would run up to her room and get her cape and hat as quietly as possible. She would have to slip down into the kitchen then and borrow an umbrella from Julia.

But Bertha, administering to Elsie, heard the door of Kate's closet when a surprising little gust of wind banged it shut while Kate was inside reaching for her hat. When Kate had fumbled for the knob and opened the door, Bertha had come into her room. At once Kate noticed that Bertha, too, was labouring under great excitement. Her cheeks were on fire and she was simply quivering with suppressed emotion of some sort.

"Oh, Miss Kate," she cried, nervously, looking at the hat in Kate's hand. "Are you going out?"

Well, no help for it now. Elsie had heard, of course. But Kate was much bothered. "Yes, on an errand. I'll be gone almost no time at all, though." This she spoke loudly, meaning that Elsie should not miss it.

"Oh, if you are really going into the village *could* you do an errand for Miss Elsie?"

Ho, ho! Was this the thin ruse Elsie meant to use, to get her out of the way?

"Perhaps," Kate said, noncommittally.

"That fixes everything nicely then." Bertha took a deep breath of relief. "I would go myself but Miss Frazier expects me to see the doctor when he comes, in order to report to her. And then there is all my work. Wait a minute."

Bertha hurried back into Elsie's room and Kate heard a low murmuring between them. When she returned she had Elsie's purse in her hand. "Here is some money. Miss Elsie says to use only that that's tied in the handkerchief."

So! Elsie was letting her pocketbook go. Last night, Kate remembered, Elsie had taken it when starting toward the door. And running away she would surely need it. Kate recalled her first motion to decline the purse and tuck the handkerchief with the coin tied in its corner into her own. With Elsie's pocketbook in her possession, Elsie was just so much the safer.

"What does she want?"

"Half a dozen eggs. A head of lettuce. Some bread."

Kate stared. Bertha stared back at her, nervously. But Kate restrained any exclamations and simply nodded. When Bertha realized that she was not going to be questioned, relief like sunshine overspread her flushed face.

"And will you be as quick as possible?" she asked.

Again Kate was pleasantly surprised. "Yes, I'll be as quick as I can," she agreed. "If Elsie will promise to stay in bed until luncheon time."

Bertha looked at her in genuine astonishment at that. "But of course. Miss Frazier has ordered that she spend the day in bed."

"No, she must promise me herself. You tell her."

Elsie had heard. She called out now, "Yes, I promise. And do please hurry, Kate."

Kate was deeply relieved. Now she could absent herself from the house without fear of finding Elsie flown when she returned. "And whatever you do, Kate Marshall, and whatever they say about it, don't let them charge those things at the store to Aunt Katherine," Elsie called again.

"You haven't an umbrella," Bertha said, bringing her Elsie's, a gay green silk one with an ivory handle. "It's a wild day for July, and I'm not at all certain Miss Frazier would like your going out like this. If you could only have the car—but it's gone to town with her."

"Yes, I know. And you needn't feel responsible. I have an errand on my own account, you know."

But Kate did wonder much about Elsie's errand. "I think," she mused, "it's a wild-goose chase Aunt Katherine is on in town, and those detectives, too. Where they *might* do some good, and find some *clues*, is right here. Who was that man in the garden? Why all this buying of groceries? If there is a snarl of some sort that needs unravelling, and if Elsie has anything to do with it, the end of the string is right here. But how do I know the snarl ought to be unravelled by detectives—that it's any of their business? Oh, heavens! I must run to the telegraph office. Mother is terribly needed this very minute."

At the Western Union Station she did not study long over the wording of her message. Time was too precious, she felt, for even a minute's delay, if Katherine was to catch the noon train from Middletown.

A mix-up here come first train nobody sick or dead KATE.

She was aware that those ten words would worry her mother unspeakably. But how, in the limits of a telegram (Kate had never conceived of the possibility of a telegram being over ten words in length!), was she to persuade her mother to take the next train if she was not to be worried? No, the only way to make absolutely sure of her coming was to frighten her into it.

The man who took the message looked at Kate curiously. He knew perfectly well who Kate was and wondered very much about the "mix-up." He thought Kate peculiarly self-contained for a young lady who found herself in a situation that necessitated that message. If he had only known, however, Kate's calm exterior was entirely assumed. She was more excited, perhaps, than she had ever been in her life before, and full of presentiments of even greater excitement to come. Sending the wire, though, was a great relief. In a few minutes Katherine herself, 'way off in quiet Ashland, would be concerned in the affair. With Katherine once "in it", Kate was assured things must somehow turn out right.

Now for those puzzling groceries.

When she came out of Holt and Holt's with her purchases, Jack Denton suddenly appeared at her shoulder. He was without an umbrella, but in a raincoat and felt hat that required none.

"May I walk along with you?" he asked.

Kate was very glad to see him. His high spirits brought relief from the strain and confusion in her mind. Gallantly, and with the air of courtesy that was so delightful in him, he took her bundles from her and then her umbrella. With laughter and exchange of party remembrances they started off together through the rain toward home.

But before they had gone half the distance Jack turned serious.

"Do you know," he said, "at our dinner last night (Mother gave a dinner before your dance) some of us decided to go on strike, to stand up for our own ideas more practically against our elders. Younger generation stuff. We all used to like Elsie tremendously, and now we are going to treat her just exactly as though nothing had happened, if she'll let us. I think she will, too. She was all right last night."

Kate turned to look up at Jack under the umbrella. The brown eyes that returned her look had lost their easy laughter and were earnest with the glow of a *cause*.

"Granny's had her way long enough," he continued. "Our mothers and fathers never really cared a bit, you know. It's just those more ancient ones. They barely survived the shock. You see *their* daughters and sons had been playing around with him, and any one of their daughters might have married him. Granny says her grandson (meaning me) is going to have the protection her daughter didn't have (meaning Mother). It's really just a joke. And we only humoured 'em because they were so rabid. Now we're sorry we were so soft. I wanted to tell you."

"I don't understand," Kate said, quickly. "Not one word. Can't you explain better? What happened that was so awful? What was the thing that shocked them so? And what has it to do with Elsie?"

Until this minute she had not wanted such information, when it came, to come from outside. She had felt that to learn that way would be disloyal of her. But now that her whole mind was turned to helping Elsie she wanted to know all she could. She wanted to get hold of the end of the tangle, any way, and perhaps then there would be some chance of straightening it out. The information that Jack was apparently able to give her would surely constitute that end; once having that in her fingers she might unravel snarl after snarl for herself.

Jack, however, was not prepared for her questions. He whistled, startled. "Don't you know what the fuss has been about?" he asked. "Don't you know about anything? I thought you were only pretending yesterday."

"No, truly. Not a thing. Aunt Katherine was surprised that I didn't know, too. But she wouldn't tell me. You tell me."

"Why, it doesn't seem fair. I thought, of course, you knew. But you did know there was something?"

"Yes, almost the first minute I got here. Elsie acted so queerly. And then she said she hardly knew you. And all the time there you were living right next door. It was puzzling. Now tell me."

"Well, if they want you to live in ignorance it's hardly up to me to enlighten you, is it?" Jack was very ill at ease.

"Your grandmother would have told me if I had let her. And Elsie herself acts as though I knew. She has accused me several times. I've wired to my mother to come. I am frightened about Elsie. She is in danger of doing—oh, something that would be dreadful for Aunt Katherine, and for herself, too. Aunt Katherine is away for the day. The more I know the more I can help. Please tell me just everything you can."

"I hate doing that. But if it helps you to help—— Anyway, it's only fair to you. You ought to know what everybody else knows. Elsie's father, Nick Frazier, is a thief. He stole some securities, or something, from Miss Frazier."

Kate did not even exclaim. She had slowed her steps for the great revelation and was now gazing straight ahead. It took some seconds for her to react at all to what Jack had said.

Jack paced on beside her, protecting her from the gusty rain by dexterous manipulations of the green silk umbrella.

"That wouldn't have been enough in itself to make them so rabid, though," he went on, worriedly. "You see they blame your aunt some. She adopted him, you know—anyway, let him call her 'aunt'—and took him into her home and prepared him herself for Harvard. He wasn't even in school. He was working in some mill in spite of being just a kid, fourteen or something like that, when she discovered him. He hadn't any family—didn't even know who his family were, had been brought up in some institution or other. Well, Miss Frazier treated him just as though he belonged to her, gave him her name and everything. This is all an old story in this village. Rose and I were brought up on it. Then when he was in college Miss Frazier expected him to be asked everywhere to holiday affairs here, and she gave parties in her house. She acted just as though he were a Frazier really. The young people liked him, though it seems he was something of a diamond in the rough, you know, 'spite of Harvard and all. But the parents grumbled. That was our grandmothers, you see. They only let it go on because your aunt was a Frazier and could do almost anything, they being such a fine old New England family. The parents always said no good would come of it, though. 'Blood would tell.'"

"Yes, yes," Kate agreed, tremulously. "That's what your grandmother said last night."

"What! Still mumbling over that? Talk about fixed ideas! When he stole those securities—he did it while your aunt was abroad or somewhere—and she let him go to prison for it, everybody said, 'Now Katherine Frazier's learned her lesson, I guess.' That was two years ago or more. But then right away his wife died, and Elsie came to live here with Miss Frazier, and Miss Frazier expected us all to treat her just as we always had when she visited before, just as though she *were* Miss Frazier's regular niece and not the daughter of a convict who doesn't even know his own name. That got the old folks' goat right enough. They said they'd tried that once on their own children. But would they let it be perpetrated on their grandchildren? You can bet, no. And there was a great to-do. And, well, we haven't been exactly cordial to Elsie."

Kate said nothing when he stopped. Jack wondered what she was thinking. He felt very hot and ashamed. "But that's all past now," he said. "Elsie isn't to blame. Why should she suffer?"

"Now I'll keep my mouth shut until she speaks," he told himself.

But Kate did not break the silence until they came to the foot of the steps leading up to Miss Frazier's front door. Then she looked up at Jack as she took her bundles from him. "Thanks for telling me everything like that," she said, gravely. "I think it's all pretty hard on Aunt Katherine and just simply awful for Elsie. No wonder she thought I was a beast. Why, I called her a 'thief' herself, and said we were being followed by that detective as though we were thieves. Now I understand a lot of things! I've—I've—just *wallowed* in *breaks*. I hope my mother gets here to-night."

"Do you play Mah Jong?" Jack asked quickly. "Why don't you and Elsie come over to play this afternoon? There's nothing much we can do out-of-doors."

"Elsie's sick in bed, so I'm afraid we can't. Thank you for carrying the things—and for everything." In spite of her perturbation she flashed her peculiar Chinese smile when Jack raised his hat. What nice manners he had!

Jack himself, walking slowly back to his own door, was obviously deep in thought. But in the midst of worrying over the ethics of what he had done in going into all that unpleasant business with Kate, he suddenly thought, "She isn't nearly so pretty as last night. But it's awfully jolly when she smiles, and I guess when she isn't being pestered with sickening scandal and such stuff she smiles a lot."

CHAPTER XVII
INTO THE ORCHARD HOUSE

Isadora opened the door for Kate as she came up the steps. There was a yellow envelope in her hand.

"A telegram for you, Miss Kate. It came just a minute ago. Oh, I do hope there's no bad news."

Kate caught a glimpse of Julia wavering at the farthest end of the hall in shadow, and there was Effie just inside the drawing-room, deliberately watching while she opened the envelope.

"I'm sure it's not bad news," Kate informed these anxious friends of her mother's as she tore open the end of the envelope. "I *expected* a wire." She felt some importance in saying that, and she was glad to clear the air, for it was charged with keenest apprehension.

Kate's message had gone and Katherine's reply arrived all within an hour. Katherine had certainly not hesitated over a decision. Kate nodded as she read and smiled.

Am autoing to Ludlow Junction to catch back way express Oakdale five-five whatever situation keep cool and brave in a few hours Mother will be with you rejoiced you're not sick. K.

Katherine certainly had not counted the words!

When Kate looked up, the anxious watchers had vanished, dispersed by her smile as she read. She sat down in a chair standing against the wall. Her arms dropped at her sides and she leaned her head against the high-carved back of the chair, crushing a little her mother's best hat. For the minute she was too absorbed in her own thoughts and too fatigued—the fatigue that is apt to come with sudden complete relief of mind—to remember such an item as a hat.

A step on the stair made her look up. Bertha was hurrying down, rustling in a raincoat, a scarf tied over her head.

"You're here," she exclaimed. "I saw you coming, from a window upstairs. Are these the things?"

Kate nodded, and Bertha took the packages and pocketbook from the floor where Kate had carelessly dropped them to tear open her telegram. Bearing them carefully she went away *through the drawing-room.*

"Well, she can't get to the kitchen that way," Kate mused, hardly caring. "And why the raincoat? Oh, well, What's the use of trying to puzzle anything out any more? Mother's coming, Mother's coming, Mother's coming!"

After a little while, yawning and half asleep, she wandered into Aunt Katherine's own sitting-room—a graceful, comfortable little retreat tucked away in an isolated corner of the big house. The outstanding feature there was an oil painting of Kate's mother at the age of sixteen in a blue party frock standing against dark velvet portières. It was a painting by Hopkinson in his earlier manner, executed with finish and most delicate feeling. The painting was one of Miss Frazier's most valuable possessions, and Kate had surmised, when her aunt had shown it to her, one of the dearest. Certainly it was a painting with a spell over it, a spell of beauty and something besides, unnamable and illusive. Perhaps it was the spirit of youth which the artist had with such genius caught there, that gave it its magic.

Kate unfolded an afghan that lay conveniently on the foot of the sofa beneath the portrait, and curling herself up under it, settled down for a nap. She felt perfectly safe in losing herself for the time because Elsie had given her promise to stay in bed until luncheon.

But at one o'clock Bertha brought down the news that the doctor had ordered Elsie to remain in bed all afternoon, too. She was asleep now, and Bertha thought she would sleep for several hours. Her temperature had gone down to normal and she was comfortable. Later, when she woke, Bertha would take her up a light meal.

Lunching alone for Kate was a rather dreary procedure in spite of the coziness of the breakfast-room where Miss Frazier had thoughtfully ordered the meal served, and the merry little fire crackling on the hearth. Kate had had a good sleep and she was now so rested in body and mind that she could think about things with some clarity. She leaned her elbow on the table and her chin in her hand and regarded the fire as though it were her companion at the meal.

Elsie's father was a thief! How would it feel to have your father a thief and in prison and everybody knowing it? Kate had never known a father, so she found it difficult to put herself in Elsie's place. But suppose it were her mother? Oh, supposing that was too painful, and certainly it wasn't like that for Elsie. Perhaps Elsie cared as little for her father as she had for her mother. (Kate had never recovered from the horrid shock of that disclosure.) She certainly never mentioned him. But she was not allowed to mention him. What had Aunt Katherine's letter said on that point? "Nick's name is not mentioned here, either by Elsie or the servants,"—something like that. But imagine consenting to forget your father for *any one*! No, of course Elsie had no such devotion for her father as Kate's for her mother. Not likely. No use to try to compare, then. Besides, the mere notion was altogether too painful.

Let's begin at the beginning, though. Why had Elsie bought bread and eggs and lettuce and nuts which she surely had no use for herself; and why had she been so urgent that Kate should buy more to-day? Surely she didn't expect to take such perishable things with her in her flight from Aunt Katherine's house! There had been no sign of eatables when Kate unpacked the runaway's suitcase last night. Oh! An idea! Had Elsie planned to run away only as far as the orchard house, and was the food supply stored there? Was that the mystery about the orchard house? Had she discovered a secret room or something and was planning to live in it like a hermit without any one's knowing? Kate built up quite a plot around that idea. It would be exciting and fascinating to live right under your guardian's nose while that guardian was scouring the country for you. But in spite of the possibilities of this story-like mystery, Kate finally let it go as an explanation. It was too far-fetched.

A better solution! Had Nick, her father, escaped from prison? Elsie was shielding him, perhaps. Why, of course, she was hiding him in the orchard house. Kate's heart began to hammer. Stupid, not to have thought of that at once, just the minute Jack told her about Elsie's father being a thief. All the food had been for him. The book she couldn't afford to buy, too! She had wanted it for him. How very simple it all was! And they were going to escape together. They would escape into Canada or somewhere. No, vague memories of something called "extradition papers" came to mind. They would simply hide themselves in the crowds of some big city. They would vanish. Oh, well, from the very first Elsie had been a vanishing comrade. When she ran away with her father she would vanish for good.

Now, how did the detective work into this solution of the puzzle? Suddenly there was a snag. If Nick had escaped from prison, wouldn't state detectives be on his trail? Mr. O'Brien, Aunt Katherine had told her, was a private detective. And if Nick had really escaped from prison surely Aunt Katherine would not in any way be concerned in finding him. That would be simply a matter for the police.

Kate turned her eyes uneasily to the open door, almost expecting to see a plain-clothes man spying upon her from the rain out there. But there was only the drenched garden and beyond, the orchard, wreathed in a haze of wet weather.

One more snag: surely if Nick had escaped from prison it would have got into the papers, and someone in Oakdale have seen it. Then Jack would know, and he had not even hinted at such a thing.

But now for the most important consideration of all: the stranger in the garden who had given her the note for Elsie last night? Who was he, and where did he come in? The reasonable answer was that he was Nick himself, Elsie's father, the thief, the man who had stolen from his own benefactress. But Kate did not harbour this idea for the fraction of a second. That voice was not the voice of such a one, and such a one would hardly be quoting from "The King of the Fairies."

Deep down in her heart, deep beyond reason, Kate had connected that stranger in the garden with what Elsie had said about fairies in the orchard house. This man himself, who had given her the note, was a human being, of course, She didn't go so far as to think him unearthly; but he might very well know about those fairies who "were in it somehow." He seemed a person who would indeed be *likely* to know. Kate was ready to connect that stranger with any mystery so long as it was a pleasant mystery. With an unpleasant mystery—never. His note had told Elsie not to run away; Elsie herself had said so. But he had known that she meant to run away. That was apparent. Where had he come from out of the wind last night?

What of that light she had seen in the orchard house her first night here? Those three open windows? That closing door in the second story—closing as though a knob had been turned?

Oh, there were just too many things to think of and to fit in. The shortest cut to clearing up some of the mystery and giving her mother a starting point to work from with Elsie when she should get here at five o'clock to-night was to explore the orchard house now, right away. There was her heart whacking at her sides again! Yes, but she must do it, escaped convict or not. That was the first step to be taken. She had the end of the string—Jack Denton had given her that—the orchard house came next, made the first knot to be untangled.

"No, no dessert, thank you." You couldn't eat with your heart hammering like that, could you? She walked to the door. The rain was stopping, had almost entirely stopped. The key was upstairs, back in the drawer of her dressing table where she had replaced it after wringing it from Elsie yesterday. If she went for it now Elsie might hear and again weep her into a promise to keep away from the orchard house. The key had been only a matter of form, anyway. There were always the windows. Kate was sure they couldn't all be locked. She would try getting in that way before she bothered about the key.

She glanced down at her rubber-soled canvas ties. No need for rubbers. No need for a sweater or umbrella, either: the little showers of rain blowing down from trees and bushes would do her chintz no harm.

She crossed the terrace, hoping neither Elsie nor Bertha was looking from a window overhead, and walked through the orchard straight to the orchard house. Before trying the windows, better try the door. That was only common sense. The latch lifted under her fingers! Had the house always stood open like this, and all that fuss about the key! She pushed the door softly open and went in.

"Something to do with fairies," Elsie had said. Kate remembered the words as she crossed the threshold. And she felt surely as though it might easily have something to do with fairies; she might have been stepping into Fairyland itself for the eerie sensation that crossing the threshold gave her.

She left the door open behind her, and a gusty wet wind followed her like a companion. It filled the hall with the pungent scent of the syringa bush by the step.

There was nothing in the hall but a little oblong table standing against the wall at the foot of the stairs, a table with curly legs and a carved top on which stood an empty card tray, and hung above the table was a narrow long mirror in a gilded frame.

Kate looked into the mirror. How many, many times it had reflected her mother's face. How very unlike Katherine her daughter was, hair bobbed so straight, rather slanting narrow eyes, full lips, freckles across the nose! Kate surveyed this image with her usual slight sense of annoyance upon meeting it in a mirror. She imagined Katherine, a Katherine of her own age, looking over her shoulder in the glass, their two heads together. It was the Katherine of the portrait, dark curly head, wide misty eyes, olive cheeks ever so delicately touched with rose.

Oh! Had that face actually gleamed out there for an instant? Her mental vision had been so clear that she could not be sure it had not, just for a flash, taken actual form.

Well, if the Katherine of sixteen years ago had joined her now and was going to accompany her in her exploration of the orchard house, so much the better. Kate had always longed for a girl comrade more than for anything else in the world. Come, let's pretend she had one at last, Katherine at fifteen.

First the parlour. It opened on the right. The door stuck. Kate pushed with her knee and lifted up on the knob simultaneously. It opened explosively. And a door up in the second story somewhere opened in sympathy with it. Kate stood very still, listening. The jarring of the walls was the cause, of course; but even with this explanation accepted, it was creepy.

The little parlour was stuffy, as all closed rooms are stuffy. But almost at once the syringa-scented air from the open front door had remedied that; it was so much more vital than the smell of dust and mildew. But why think of the parlour as "little," for by any ordinary standards it was certainly a good-sized room. Only in comparison with Aunt Katherine's spacious drawing-room did Kate feel it now small and quaint.

The furniture was much as it had been left when Grandfather Frazier died and the house was closed. But the books were gone from the low bookcases that lined the walls. Those Aunt Katherine had sent to her niece, and Kate had grown up in their company.

The bookcases, a Franklin stove with a worn low bench in front of it, a big square library table between the windows, some oil paintings on the walls (Kate guessed some of these to be Aunt Katherine's work), a comfortable-looking but very unfashionable chintz-covered sofa, and several very shabby, very welcoming easy chairs with deep seats and wide arms and curving backs—that was the parlour.

And the fifteen-year-old Katherine Frazier had gone in ahead of Kate. She was moving about the room, poking up the fire (the fire that didn't exist) in the grate, throwing her school books on the sofa, reading absorbedly curled up with her feet under her in the deepest chair by the window, making toast at the coals in the grate while the blue teapot kept itself warm on the stove's top. Katherine had told Kate about this room, how she loved it and what she did in it. Her father was there usually in the picture, too, and often Aunt Katherine. But somehow Kate imagined neither of them now.

What a merry, comfortable, *spirited* room it was. Its spirit had been created by that dark-eyed girl. And the smell of the syringa! Now Kate knew why her mother could never get by the syringa bush at the corner of Professor Hart's lawn without stopping for deep breaths when the syringa was in flower.

The dining-room was across the hall. The dining table was long and narrow, the handicraft of Great-grandfather Frazier. It was curly maple and mirror-like with the polishings of many years. Close at one end two chairs were drawn up to it. Several more stood with their backs against the wall. Did Grandfather Frazier and Katherine sit close together like that at the end of the long table those years they lived alone? Kate wondered. Yes, she was sure they did; for there was the Katherine of her imagination pouring tea for her father and handing it to him with a sweet, affectionate smile. No need for Nora to come in from the kitchen to pass it. This father and daughter could reach each other.

The kitchen failed to hold Kate's attention. She missed Katherine there. The young Katherine had not liked housework. Indeed, it was still a burden to her, however gracefully she carried the burden. Perhaps that was why Kate could not find her in the kitchen.

If stepping across the threshold into this empty house had stirred Kate's imagination and made her feel the possibility of fairies hiding somewhere in the apparent emptiness, going up the stairs stirred it even more.

It was a steep, rather narrow, little staircase, painted black and with the wooden treads deeply worn by generations of feet. And right in the very middle of her ascent, on the seventh stair, to be precise, there happened to her a thing that had sometimes happened before but never quite so *definitely*. She thought and felt that she had done this all before, that she had come up these stairs on exactly the errand she was on now; she remembered herself on this identical stair, with her hand on this identical portion of the railing. More than that she knew exactly what was going to happen to her when she reached the top—why shouldn't she know when she had experienced it all before?

But even as she felt this and in fact knew it, her foot had left that seventh stair and the memory had vanished. Now she only had a memory of a memory, or to be exact not even that. She only remembered that she *had* remembered. The instant itself, the connection, was lost.

She looked into the guest-room first. It was a pretty room in spite of the absence of curtains and bedding. The furniture was painted a creamy yellow. Katherine had painted it a few days before her marriage. By the window there was a dainty little writing table with pens and blotters and even ink-bottle conveniently placed. But the ink had been long evaporated and the pens were rusty. Above the bed there hung, passe-partouted in white, a flower-wreathed quotation. Had Aunt Katherine or her mother painted the flowers and illuminated the letters? The flowers were morning-glories, very realistically done, and the quotation from "Macbeth": "Sleep that knits up the ravelled sleave of care."

"Morning-glories are incongruous with the words," Kate mused, smiling. She felt more sophisticated than the fifteen-year-old Katherine who had admired this crude bit of art enough to hang it in the guest-room, who perhaps was even herself its perpetrator. "Yes, morning-glories are incongruous with the words."

"*Are they. Why?*"

"Perhaps they aren't," Kate answered, aloud. She remembered her flight that very morning toward the slowly opening many-coloured portals of sleep. Morning-glories might very well be growing on Sleep's walls.

But whom had she answered? Who had spoken? No one, of course. There was no one there *to* speak, except Kate herself.

On either side the hall there was another bedroom. Kate merely looked in at their doors. One had been her mother's, and it was entirely bare now, for all the furniture had gone to the barn-house in Ashland years ago. The other had been Grandfather Frazier's room, and somehow Kate felt that she did not want to pry there. It would be like getting acquainted with him when his back was turned.

Now there remained only the "playroom" and the upstairs "study"—a long room at the back of the house, the room where the windows had stood open that first night of Kate's arrival—and ever since, for all she knew. From her very first entrance into the house Kate had been *listening* toward this room. It was in that room she fully expected to discover Elsie's secret. It was really the goal of her pilgrimage through the house. But the nearer she drew to it physically the more she drew back mentally. She was not exactly frightened. What did not frighten Elsie need not frighten her. It was simply uneasiness in the face of mystery.

There was the playroom between, though. Kate was grateful to pause a minute in the playroom.

The playroom was down a step, through a little low door. Kate had to bend her head to go through the door. It was the smallest room she had ever been in, about the size of a goodly closet. Shelves were built in all around the walls, leaving space only for the one little low window that reached the floor. Before the shelves, strung on brass rings to brass rods, hung dusty, faded calico curtains, yellow flowers on a blue background. Kate pushed back a curtain, jangling all its rings. The shelves held a jumble of toys, birds, beasts, carts, engines, and on the top shelf a row of dolls, some broken almost beyond recognition as dolls, but two or three still healthy bisque beauties smiling blandly over her head at the opposite wall.

There were three lilliputian chairs in the room, one a black rocker painted on the back and seat with flowers and fruit. In one corner there was a huge box of blocks, wooden building blocks that Great-grandfather Frazier had made for Grandfather Frazier when he was a little boy.

Kate knelt by that box, and idly began constructing a house. She had always adored building with blocks when she was a little girl, and now the old fascination seized her; besides, she was putting off the minute when she would open the door of that last room.

But as she completed the second wall of the house she turned suddenly and looked over her shoulder. Had she heard something? A rustling, like a dress coming down the hall and pausing at the door of the playroom? Whom did she expect to see bending down at the low door and looking in at her where she sat on the floor building with blocks like a little girl? Strangely, it was not the sixteen-year-old Katherine she had been imagining as her companion whom she pictured stooping down at that door to look in. It was Katherine's mother, Kate's grandmother, who had died when Katherine was still a little girl playing with blocks. Only she would not look like an ordinary grandmother, of course. For she had died when she was only twenty-four. She was a young woman, very graceful, very gentle, lovely.

Of course she wasn't really there at the door, wondering who had come in her baby's stead to play in the playroom. Of course she wasn't there with a spray of syringa flower at her belt. It was just Kate's vivid imagination. She was sensible enough to know that. The rustling of her dress had been the leaves of the drenched apple tree boughs against the window pane tossed by a rainy breeze. And the syringa scent had followed Kate up here and even down into the little playroom.

It was a low little room, so low that Kate could but just stand up straight in it. And it was entirely bare except for the shelves with their treasure trove of toys, the box of blocks, and the lilliputian chairs. But for all that the room was alive to Kate now. It was almost giddy with life. And it was a life that did not concern her. She was an intruder. She became uneasy as intruders are uneasy.

But she was not driven away precipitately. She stayed long enough to replace the blocks in their place coolly. Then, still coolly, she stood up and went out of the playroom, closing the door softly after her.

In the hall, however, she allowed herself to hurry. The door to the last room, the study, was ajar. Had the figure of Kate's imagination gone on ahead to that room—the young mother? For an instant Kate hesitated with her fingers on the knob.

"Psha! What are you afraid of! Silly!"

Downstairs, the hall door, which she had left open, blew shut with a bang, A fresh downpour of rain rattled on the shingles just above her head. (There was no attic above this part of the house.) Kate's impulse was to run down and secure at least the staying open of the front door, so that she might have an unimpeded exit in case of panic. The door fastened open, she would come back and have the fun of discovering for herself Elsie's secret which was the mystery of the orchard house.

But Kate did not follow her impulse. Instead, she squared her shoulders, lifted her head a little defiantly, and pushed back that last door. She stepped in.

"Oh! Oh!" But it was not a shriek. It was just a soft "oh! oh!" of purest astonishment. For the room was occupied; but not by the ghost of her grandmother.

CHAPTER XVIII
THE LAST ROOM

A man was sitting leaning forward over a table with his back to the three windows, his face toward the door. His arms were spread out on the table, his hands clasped. He leaned there waiting for something. It was Kate for whom he had been waiting, for he had heard every movement of hers almost since her first light step on the porch.

Kate stood now, smiling at him across the room. Her sudden smile following upon her amazed "Oh! Oh!" surprised him almost as much as his being there at all surprised her. He was prepared for her being startled, angry, accusing, anything except charmed. On the tip of his tongue there waited a reassuring word. That was why he had not risen when she entered; he wanted to avoid any movement that might frighten her. But all his careful precaution was wasted. Kate was not frightened. She was charmed, purely and simply charmed.

"Why, you are the boy," she exclaimed, "the boy in the dragony, flowery picture frame!"

But even as she spoke she realized that although it was the boy indeed, it was the boy grown older. The crisp curly hair was clipped very short and was almost entirely gray. And there were deep lines about his eyes and nose and mouth. The light in the face had grown, too, that peculiar light betokening gaiety of the spirit and sympathy. Yes, it was truly the boy, only the boy *more so*, in spite of lines and gray hair.

"The dragony, flowery picture frame?" he repeated after her in the voice of the stranger in the garden.

He had spoken. He was real. Not just another one of her fancies.

"Yes, in the top drawer of Mother's desk. That boy. Only excuse me, I thought I was talking to a dream. Are you real?"

The man laughed, a very jolly laugh, and nodded.

"Did Mother know you would be here? Is that why she insisted that I come into the orchard house the first minute I could?"

He shook his head. "No, she couldn't know I would be here."

He stood up then. But as he moved Kate noticed that he took special care to stand between the windows where he could not be seen by any one who might be in the orchard.

"You have made a mistake," he said. "I don't think I can be the person you think. My picture wouldn't be in your mother's desk."

But Kate nodded, perfectly sure of her facts.

"Oh, yes, you are. Mother's always had you. You've been our talisman for years, both of ours. And that's funny, for neither of us knew about the other's feeling until just before I came away."

His face had reddened. "Her talisman?" he asked, incredulously.

"Just as much hers as mine. It was very funny. But it's even funnier—of course I don't mean funny, I mean strange—that I've found you here."

"But don't you know who I am?" the man asked.

"Only that you're the talisman. I don't know your name."

"Exactly. Your mother didn't want you even to know his name. Well, time justified her. It fulfilled all their prophecies. He was a nobody first and a convict afterward. No wonder she didn't tell you his name."

Kate looked at him steadily, trying to take it in, to connect it up. He went on:

"Your mother didn't tell you his name because it is the same as hers. She is too ashamed. I am Nick Frazier. Now you know."

The words sounded bitter, but the man's manner belied them. He said it all with a friendly smile, seeming more concerned that Kate should get things straight and not be too shocked than airing personal bitterness. But Kate protested.

"No, no. She did you some wrong once. That is why she couldn't talk about you to me. But she did say that she knew it would come right sometime. She wouldn't talk about it. So I mustn't. But you know it isn't at all as you say. She isn't ashamed of you at all."

After a minute's thought she added, "If you're that boy, and you are, then she didn't know anything about—about——"

"That I am a thief?"

"Yes. Jack Denton told me that this morning. Well, I'm sure she didn't know that. And now I remember she said she had no idea why you and Aunt Katherine had quarrelled. She was puzzled by that in the letter asking me to come. She didn't even know Elsie was living here. She didn't know anything about you at all."

"Listen, Kate." Nick spoke rapidly. "Tell your mother when you go back all that Jack Denton told you. But tell her, too, that it isn't so black, not quite so black as it sounds. And tell her that all the King of the Fairies taught those two kids in the orchard I have learned since I went to prison. For I wrote 'The King of the Fairies.' I wrote it in prison, thinking everything over. Tell her I shall never again accept another penny from any one or let any one help me. What I took from your aunt I'm paying back to-day with the royalties on the book. Will you remember to tell her that?"

Kate nodded. Yes, certainly she would remember. But her whole mind was taken up with delight that he, the boy in the dragony, flowery picture frame, was the author of their precious book. That was what mattered most, in this minute, to her.

He saw that she was not impressed with the fact of his having been a convict. That he was her talisman come alive, and the author of "The King of the Fairies," both at once, was tremendous enough to wipe out all the rest.

"Elsie's father wrote 'The King of the Fairies,' that book! And she never told me!"

Kate sat on the edge of the table and bombarded him with questions. He answered them all. There were places that had puzzled even her mother in the book. He clarified them for Kate now. "My new book is *clearer*," he said. "I am learning better how to say what I want to say."

"Your new book! There is another!"

"Yes, it will be published this fall." He told her about that. She was enthralled. She clasped her hands and listened, the corners of her mouth tilting up like wings.

Then it was her turn to talk. Nick was the sort of person who draws you out. In all her life Kate had never experienced such sympathy in a human being. That was Nick's rare gift. She told him the story of her life, quite literally, at least, from the year she was seven, beginning with the day of her sharpest memory when she and her mother saw the fairy by the spring. It was very much on her mind now because of that experience at Madame Pearl's and she told it all to Nick in detail. "How can it be explained?" she asked. "How could Elsie be just exactly that fairy?"

"That's a hard question," he agreed. "But if there's anything in what these fourth dimensional experts are saying—then it might be explained reasonably enough, even mathematically. You know they say time *is* the fourth dimension. Well, in that instant in the woods, they might say, you got somehow into a four-dimension world."

But Kate did not understand. Nick came from his station between the windows and sat on the edge of the table beside her, forgetting the hypothetical somebody in the orchard, and went into the subject more deeply. Kate followed his reasoning for a time, almost as though she were beginning to grasp something of the meaning of it all, when, bang! She slipped back to her first position of ignorance. She didn't understand a bit.

Nick laughed. "It's exactly the same with me," he confessed. "I get a little farther than you do now in grasping it perhaps, and then 'bang!' just as you say, I lose the steps by which I got there. However, we can know that science itself is working toward some such explanation for that fairy by the spring of yours and its like."

"And so you don't believe in fairies at all? I was really only looking into the future, at Elsie as she would be years away, in that mirror of Madame Pearl's?"

"Nonsense. Just because we have reason to believe that what you saw wasn't a fairy—since it was Elsie and couldn't be—proves no case against the existence of fairies. Does it? Yes, I believe in fairies right enough, but that's a matter of faith with me rather than reasonable conviction."

It was all very fascinating. Nick led Kate's mind a race, and she felt as though she were "expanding." She called it "expanding" when telling her mother of it later. Why, Nick did to you exactly what his book did, pushed roofs skyward and walls horizon-ward. And all the while he was so jolly. He laughed and made you laugh often, laughter with a special quality of joy in it.

But suddenly, right in the midst of everything, he looked at his watch. "Do you know, it's after five," he said, "and I——"

Kate interrupted what he was about to say. "After five! Why, Mother may be here already! I forgot about time! How could I!"

"Your mother? Here!"

"Yes, I telegraphed her to come."

Kate had quite forgotten her anxieties about Elsie, and how much she had imagined her in need of Katherine's sympathy and help. Now everything came back with a rush. "I must run."

But Nick caught at her hand before she could run. "Kate!" he said, excitedly. "Why didn't you tell me?" Then he became calm, but still held Kate back by the hand. He spoke very earnestly.

"Bring her out here. Your aunt isn't at home. No one need know. I must see her. Will you bring her? Tell her it may be our very last chance to meet ever. Tell her that and *make* her come."

Kate looked into the face so suddenly become passionately earnest and said in surprise, "But of course she will want to come."

But as she sped through the orchard it occurred to her that she had solved nothing, got nowhere, or almost nowhere, in the mystery. What was Nick doing in the orchard house? Was he a fugitive from the law? Somehow, though she had begun to wonder again, she was not a bit bothered. Nick was Nick. Who wanted more?

Katherine had arrived in a taxi from the station a few minutes earlier and presented herself anxiously at Miss Frazier's door. She had no trepidations about meeting her aunt now, no thought of their standing quarrel. Her whole mind was taken up with her daughter. To say that she was worried would be to describe her state of mind weakly. She was very nearly frantic. She had read and reread Kate's telegram on an average of once every five minutes since its arrival, and in spite of all this study was no nearer guessing at the nature of the "mix-up" than she had been after the first reading.

Isadora was not one of the servants who had known and loved Katherine, and so it is not surprising that when she opened the door and saw her standing there with her suitcase she took her for an agent. Katherine did not enlighten Isadora as to her identity, for she wanted to see Kate first of all, and for the present Kate only. She made this very plain, and then walked past Isadora and into the drawing-room with such an air that in spite of the old black velvet tam and general lack of style in the caller's clothes, Isadora accorded her all due respect and went in search of Kate.

But Kate was not to be found in the house. Would the caller wait? Yes? Very well. Isadora withdrew with several curious backward glances.

As soon as Isadora was out of the way Katherine went through the French doors on to the terrace. She paced back and forth, looking toward the orchard house. Was Kate there? Had she forgotten the time? The maid Isadora had appeared calm and collected enough. There certainly was a sense of peace in the house. The "mix-up" perhaps was not such a desperate one, after all. Katherine couldn't wait here, though, doing nothing—not after all those hours of waiting on the train. She walked across the terrace and down into the garden toward the orchard house. She met Kate just at the edge of the trees.

Kate returned her mother's embrace and kiss almost absently. Then Katherine held her off and looked at her. "You look all right," she said, breathlessly. "Kate, tell me nothing dreadful has happened. Tell me you *are* all right. Quick!"

"Yes, yes. Oh, Mother, don't look like that! I am perfectly all right. It's about *Elsie*. But even that's all right now. Mother, her father is here. Nick is in the orchard house. He wants to see you. He says it may be the last time you ever see each other. He wants you to come right now."

But if Kate's words reassured Katherine about Kate's safety, they flung her into a new anxiety. "Nick? The last time? Why?"

"Oh, I don't know. Only come." Kate pulled at her mother's hand.

Nick had come down the stairs and was waiting in the hall. When Katherine followed Kate dazedly in, and she and Nick stood facing each other, he exclaimed involuntarily; to him it was as though the girl of eighteen he had known years ago had come back. In the black velvet tam, raindrops sparkling in her hair that waved so softly at her ears and brow, raindrops drenching her eyelashes, her face vivid with emotion, her hands outstretched to him—why, she was as young and fresh as Kate herself, more beautiful even than he had remembered her.

"I must talk with you." He was very intense and at the same time shy.

"Yes, of course. Of course we must talk." Katherine's tone implied, "Why not? Why shouldn't we?"

"In the parlour, then. I'll put up a window. No, I can't do that. Someone in the house might see."

"But why shouldn't someone see? I don't understand."

"There's air enough from the door now. Smell the syringa!"

Katherine was standing in the window, her back to them. Kate knew it was to hide strange tears. "The smell of the syringa did that," she thought, with her quick understanding where her mother was concerned. "Smells are funny that way."

Nick spoke to Kate then, with gentle imperativeness.

"Elsie will be coming out here in a minute. Yes, we are running away, if you like. Go to her and tell her to wait. Tell her we will go surely to-night, but she is to wait until your mother comes in. You keep her, Kate—stay with her— *until your mother comes in.*"

"I don't think I could. She will be furious with me. She wouldn't do what I said."

"I'll write her a note. She will understand that I want it."

He pulled an envelope from his pocket and scrawled a sentence, holding the paper against the wall. Katherine had taken off her coat and was now sitting in the deep chair in the window. Her tears had vanished, if there really had been tears, and her eyes were clear as happiness itself.

But Kate was anxious as she hurried with the note to Elsie. If Elsie had hated her before for interfering now she would hate her all the more.

She was sitting on the window seat in her room, dressed in the green silk suit and brown straw hat, a bright green raincoat thrown over a chair back near, and the suitcase of last night at her feet. Had she seen Kate come from the orchard house and return there with her mother? It was obvious that she had, for the face she turned to Kate was wild and strained.

"What have you been doing now?" she asked as Kate came into the room. "Who was that girl you took into the orchard house?"

"That wasn't a girl. It was my mother."

"Your mother! Why?"

"Your father wanted to talk to her. He sent you this."

Elsie took the note and her face lost some of its wildness as she read. When she looked up she was puzzled but almost serene.

"It's all right. We're going away just the same," she said. "Nothing can stop us now. I'm only to wait until your mother comes in."

Kate nodded. If it was her father Elsie was running away with, she, Kate, had no more responsibility. She didn't see how it was fair to Aunt Katherine or in any way right for them to do it that way, but she had no doubt that somehow it could be explained. Once understood, there would be no question of its rightness. So she put all that aside.

She said, "Oh, Elsie, why didn't you tell me your father wrote 'The King of the Fairies'? Your very own father!"

"So you know now? He told you? Well, now you know, then, that I didn't lie. There *was* something of fairy in the orchard house; Father had finished his new book there. It's all fairies."

"And you are going away now, for good? Before Aunt Katherine comes back?"

"If you will let me." Needless to say this was spoken sarcastically.

"But of course. Now that I've seen your father! No harm can come to you now, not when you've got our talisman, alive, real, to look after you."

Elsie looked at Kate, puzzled. "What do you mean? Your talisman? You do say the queerest things!"

Then Kate told her about the boy in the silvery, dragony, flowery picture frame. When she had finished, it was a new Elsie that faced her.

"And your mother, too, felt like that?"

"Yes, Mother, too. Why not?"

"Why—because——"

CHAPTER XIX
ELSIE CONFIDES

The girls stayed there, sitting on the window seat, for over an hour, watching for Katherine to come from the orchard. It was showering again, sheets of rain silvering the gardens and drawing curtains of silver magic about the orchard, swirling them all about the orchard's borders. There was plenty of time for the story which Elsie told haphazardly and in broken sentences, led on by Kate's interest, and her assurances that now she had seen Nick she would never try to interfere with any of their plans again. Kate's story of the dragony, flowery picture frame had knocked all Elsie's guards flat, too. Her story, straightened out, was this:

Elsie's earliest memory was of her father. She had fallen down the house steps and bumped her head. Nick, her father, had appeared as by magic to kiss the hurt away and run back into the house with her in his arms. She remembered him bending over her, washing the bruise with cold water; then came the smell of witch-hazel. And though this was her first conscious memory, still the very memory itself held in it the inevitableness of this comfort from her father; so she was used to his ministrations.

The next memory was convalescence after measles when she was four. She was sitting up in a chair in a window over the street, wrapped in an eiderdown. Her father was reading to her from "The Psalms of David." The words sang a beautiful song to her, especially when he came to "The Lord is my Shepherd." And it was very comforting to have her father sitting there so quietly, near her, as though he meant to stay a long time.

"But your mother?" Kate asked her. "Didn't she read to you after measles, too? Don't you remember her?"

Yes, Elsie remembered her mother, though she thought it was a later memory, and it was never a memory of *mothering*. Gloria had hummed in and out of the house like a humming-bird. Later, when Elsie saw a humming-bird for the first time, she felt as she watched it exactly as she had always felt watching her mother; and the pains that she took not to startle the little spirit away were exactly the pains she had always taken not to startle her mother away, when by chance she hummed near. Gloria looked like a humming-bird, as well as acted like one. Humming-birds fascinated Elsie, and her mother had always entranced her with the same fascination, no more.

But sometimes the humming-bird scolded at her father, pecked at him, hummed all about him pecking. Then Elsie would run away, not fascinated any more. The scolding was always about money. Gloria needed money just as a humming-bird needs honey, and often there wasn't enough.

They lived in New York near Washington Square. Elsie was cared for by nurses—such a fast-marching procession of nurses in the same chic blue uniforms, provided by the humming-bird, that Elsie remembered them as "nurse," not as individuals. Her father was the constant human factor in her life, the one person to be counted on. Gloria was merely a dash of colour beyond the nursery door somewhere, a shrill sweet voice at the piano, a swish of silk on the stairs.

At eight, Elsie was sent to boarding school. But the school was in New York, and so her father still saw her almost every day, and on Saturdays he gave her and sometimes her friends "treats." He took them to the theatre or picture galleries, or for beautiful walks in Central Park. Her mother never came to the school, but had her home once a month on Sundays for dinner. This was a grief to Elsie, not because she felt any need of her mother but simply because she would have been proud to show her schoolmates what a magnificent and fashionable mother she had; also she was humiliated by their curious questionings and pretended doubts as to whether she had a real mother at all. But Elsie was sure that her father was better than twenty mothers. She wouldn't take a mother as a gift except for show purposes.

Kate writhed at Elsie's harshness. "Oh, you don't know, Elsie! Don't talk so! How can you? It is terrible."

"That's what Ermina said when I talked to her about my mother. Ermina was my best friend, but she didn't stay out her first year at school. Her mother died, and she went home for the funeral and never came back. I knew that she loved her mother just as much as I loved my father. I hid away in my room when they told me her mother had died. I pretended I was sick. It was awful. But when I heard her go downstairs, at the very last minute while they were saying 'good-bye' to her at the door, I rushed down in my nightgown. I kissed her and hugged her and we cried terribly. Miss Putnam, the principal of the school, never forgave me for having made Ermina cry when she had been brave and not cried at all before, and for having disgraced the school by standing in the door in my nightgown. But I have been glad ever since. I had to say 'good-bye' and that I was sorry. And I don't think crying out loud was any worse than the crying *inside* that Ermina must have been doing. Do you?"

Kate agreed with Elsie. She, too, was glad Elsie had gone to her friend in her sorrow, even if she had waited till the last minute for the courage.

Vacations had been spent either at camps or at Aunt Katherine's. When they were spent at Aunt Katherine's, her father was usually with her, having a vacation, too. And those were beautiful times.

Then, when she was twelve, came the terrible time. Nick had done badly in business. He confided this to Elsie because Gloria only wanted happy confidences, and besides, she was abroad, travelling with a party of friends. There was enough to pay his debts and leave him clear to start fresh, avoiding bankruptcy. But the debts paid, and his checking account reduced to zero, money must come from somewhere to go on with until business picked up. He knew a way in which two thousand dollars, if he only had it, could overnight be turned into ten thousand. He told Elsie about it, walking in Central Park, and said if he had only waited a little to pay his debts, and not acted so hastily in his fear of bankruptcy, everything would have been made right now. Aunt Katherine would loan him the two thousand, he felt sure, if he could only explain the nature of the speculation to her. But she was travelling somewhere in England, and there would never be time to get into touch with her. But he had the key to her safety vault in her Boston bank. He suddenly told Elsie that he was going to Boston and would not see her again until Sunday. She understood that he was going to borrow, on his own account, two thousand dollars from Aunt Katherine overnight, trusting to her unfailing generosity.

Nick wrote Aunt Katherine all about it on the train as he went. From the vault he took two thousand dollars' worth of securities which could easily be replaced.

Aunt Katherine sailed for home before Nick's troubled letter reached her in England, and the second letter, telling how the two thousand instead of blossoming into ten thousand had disappeared altogether, was never sent, because just as Nick was going out of his door to post it, the cablegram came announcing Gloria's tragic death. That put all thoughts of the letter out of his mind, and when he did remember it he thought he had posted it as he meant to. It was found in the apartment months later by the people who sublet the place furnished, and simply dropped into a post box by them and sent to its address in England. It did not reach Miss Frazier until six months later.

Miss Frazier on her arrival in Boston, and after a visit to her bank, reported the missing securities to the police. Nick's immediate apprehension followed. Miss Frazier was on a train bound for California when that most amazing bit of news reached her by telegram. She was shocked almost beyond reason, and so horrified that it was impossible for her to find any justification for her adopted nephew. She offered him no help and had no words for him that were not bitter ones, but she did write to offer his "innocent child" a home with her on the condition that she should not speak her father's name for the term of his imprisonment, or correspond with him while she was in her care. That letter ended, "If I had been one half as level-headed as my niece Katherine or Mrs. Van Vorst-Smith about you, Nicholas, I should have protected you against such temptation, and we might have all been spared this catastrophe."

In Elsie's parting from her father he had shown her this letter. (Now Kate knew why Elsie had grown cold always at mention of Katherine!) He had begged her to accept her aunt's conditions. Indeed there was nothing else she could do, for her mother's relations were now more estranged from them than ever. They had not written one word, even bitter ones.

"Oh, Elsie! That must have been dreadful, not being allowed even to speak of your father, to act as though he were dead!"

Elsie looked at her, her eyes black with remembered grief. "It was. I was so lonely for him, Kate, I expected to *die*."

In time Nick's two letters about the "overnight loan," forwarded and reforwarded, had arrived in Oakdale. Then Aunt Katherine began to understand a little how his deed had not been so pitchy black as it had seemed in the first shock. He had done what she had always wanted him to do, counted on her understanding and generosity. It had been a crime—even Nick had accepted that judgment from the very first—and an utterly foolish and desperate deed, but now Aunt Katherine was sorry she had not lifted a hand to keep him from paying the penalty of imprisonment. She looked about to see what could be done, and ultimately was able to set wheels in motion that brought about his release at the end of two years instead of three. But she had not told Elsie. She had not been able to bring herself to speak of Elsie's father to her at all.

Nick wrote Miss Frazier asking her to meet him at a certain spot on the Common in Boston the day he was to be released. He wanted to discuss Elsie and what they were to do about her. He knew that his appearance in Oakdale would cause Miss Frazier painful embarrassment. He meant to avoid that for her. But when he had waited for hours at the place he had designated and she had not come, he had grown desperate. He was obsessed with a fear that Elsie might be sick. Why, she might be dead, almost, for all he knew. He had not had one word from her in two years. He boarded a train, not stopping to leave his suitcase at a hotel or check it in the South Station, and started for Oakdale.

Elsie was just coming down the steps of Aunt Katherine's house as her father got out of the taxi he had hired to avoid being seen in Oakdale and to gain speed to his destination. Aunt Katherine was away and most of the servants, for it was Thursday afternoon—a week ago last Thursday. Father and daughter had longed to be alone, unobserved by any curious eyes. The orchard house occurred to them as the best place to talk. They went around the house and managed to reach it, unseen, through the gardens. They had climbed in at a window at the back. Elsie was beside herself with happiness, and Nick was like a boy in his joy and relief about her.

He told Elsie that the first year in prison he had written "The King of the Fairies."

"There was so much in it that he had told me about the 'other side of things' and the *more* life that even stones have that we don't see, that when the book was published and I looked into it at the bookshop I knew right away it must be Father's. He had always wanted to write. At the very first sentence I knew. It was like a letter from him. I read it and read it and read it. Do you wonder I didn't want you to snatch it for yourself that very first morning, Kate?"

The second book was almost finished when Nick came out of prison. Only a chapter remained. The publishers had promised an advance on the royalties as soon as the manuscript was sent them. The first book had already made over two thousand dollars. So the two decided, between them, that Nick should live in the orchard house for a week, long enough to finish the book, send it to the publishers and get their check. Then he would leave the two thousand dollars, the earnings from the first book, for Aunt Katherine. That was exactly what he had taken from her vault. With the new check of five hundred dollars, he and Elsie would go away together. He could write in the orchard house undisturbed, and without any one's knowing he was there. Elsie could bring him some food now and then. But they would not run away together until he could leave the two thousand that really belonged to Aunt Katherine behind them.

Kate interrupted there. "But how can you! How can you treat Aunt Katherine so?"

"It's this way. I've made Father see that she doesn't like me. She is awfully kind, but that's not liking. If I vanish, it will be just a relief to her. But she wouldn't let me go, probably, if I told her. She would argue and try to keep me because it was her duty. Even Father sees that. Well, the new check has come. That was my special delivery yesterday. Father wrote Aunt Katherine a long letter and put the two thousand dollars in checks from his publishers into it. I've pinned the letter to her pincushion for her to read when she gets back to-night. Father hopes you'll stay on here and your mother come back, too, and everything be set right at last. We don't belong in the Frazier family at all, you know. We are sort of vagabonds, different, Father and I. Father thinks the quarrel between Aunt Katherine and your mother was in some way because of him. When we vanish, it will come right."

"Oh, but it won't, and it wasn't, and you aren't. Imagine you a vagabond!" Kate exclaimed.

"That's the beautiful clothes Aunt Katherine gives me. They make me look just like anybody. But really underneath I belong in a tent or something like that. Anyway, I'd rather tramp the country with my father than live in a palace with any one else!"

Kate leaned toward her, taking her hand, not timidly now but with assurance. "So would I," she agreed, heartily. "So would any one, he's so splendid and wonderful. And we are friends now, you and I, aren't we? Will you write to me when you have gone?"

Tears brimmed Elsie's eyes. "Really? Do you want me to write? Of course I will. Let's be best friends, chums. Even when I'm in California!"

Kate was embarrassed by the tears, but she was enraptured, too. She was tingling with happiness, for she was face to face with the vanishing comrade at last.

"Why didn't we feel this way sooner?" she asked with reason.

"That was my fault. I'm sorry now."

The girls had almost forgotten why they were watching the rain-curtained orchard. But they were recalled sharply to the affairs of the minute by Effie's voice in the hall not far from their door. She was calling down a stairway to Isadora.

"Tell Julia Miss Frazier's just come in and will be here for dinner, after all."

The girls started. Elsie sprang to her feet. Kate still had her hand. "Don't worry," she said, quickly. "I will help you to get out without her seeing. You can go later to-night."

"But Father's note! Pinned to her pincushion! She will read it now! Oh, why did she come back!"

"I'll go to her room and try to get the note before she notices it," Kate offered. "You just wait here. I'll do my best."

"It's on top of the tall bureau against the wall between the windows. Oh, do you suppose you *can*, Kate?"

As Kate hurried through the passageways toward Miss Frazier's bedroom she wondered whether she really could. What excuse should she give for disturbing Aunt Katherine while she was dressing?

There was no time to think that out. Aunt Katherine called "Come," almost before Kate's knuckles tapped the door.

CHAPTER XX
A FAREWELL IN THE DARK

Miss Frazier was sitting before her dressing table attired in a blue silk dressing-robe.

"Nothing the matter, Kate?" she asked, the minute that she realized it was Kate and not one of the servants who had entered. "Bertha tells me Elsie is better. I am glad I was able to get back for dinner, after all. Both you and Elsie have been on my mind. Was it a dull day?"

"No, not dull a bit." If Aunt Katherine only knew how very far from dull!

Aunt Katherine put down the comb with which she had been "fluffing" her hair. She looked at Kate questioningly. Why was her niece here, and looking so discomfited, at the dressing hour?

Kate had already spied the note, across the room, pinned to the pincushion on the bureau's top. To the corner of her eye it appeared as big as a flag! How had Miss Frazier ever avoided seeing it? It fairly shrieked in the room.

"Well?" Her aunt was expecting something of her. She must say something to make her presence reasonable. But what excuse could she ever make to go 'way across the big room to that bureau? In this plight Kate blurted out the news that her mother was there.

"Your mother!"

Aunt Katherine seemed frozen for an instant in her surprise.

"Not exactly here, but she will be in a few minutes, I think," Kate stumbled on. "I wired for her to come."

"Why, Kate! Has anything gone wrong to-day? Elsie——"

"No, nothing. Oh, I can't tell you now. Will you wait a little while, until she's here? I can't explain anything yet."

"What time is she arriving?"

Kate put her hand into her pocket and pulled out the yellow telegram. "Here, this tells," she said, vaguely. Now, oh, now while Aunt Katherine was studying out that long message was the time to rescue Elsie's letter. Kate made a move toward the bureau. But Miss Frazier moved with her! Her lorgnette lay beside the pincushion! Was there ever such luck!

She picked it up, and read, moving the glass along the paper.

She passed over the ambiguity to her of most of the message and fastened her attention upon the time of arrival stated there. "Five-five!" she exclaimed.

"The train must be over an hour late. More than that. It's half-past six now. Ring the bell, please, Kate, and tell Isadora to send Timothy to the station. He knows your mother and will bring her up here in the car when the train does get in. That back-way train is seldom on schedule, but this is unusually late. Tell Isadora to have an extra place laid, too."

Kate went over to the door and rang the servants' bell there. Bertha, not Isadora, answered. Kate stepped out into the hall and whispered quickly, "Tell Effie to set another place. My mother will be here for dinner." The directions for Timothy were, of course, not given. Then Kate went back to her aunt, with how beating a heart!

Aunt Katherine was standing with her face turned away, reading Nick's letter. Kate never thought of fleeing. She stayed stock still, waiting for the storm, and deciding that even now Aunt Katherine need not know that Elsie had not yet gone. Kate expected something quite scenic from her aunt's temper. Katherine had warned her that it was rare but devastating.

After ages and æons, to Kate's tense mind, Aunt Katherine folded the letter, check and all. Then their eyes met. The one thing that the expression in her aunt's eyes told Kate was that she was surprised, though *glad*, to find her still there. She stretched both her hands to her.

"Kate, Kate," she said with a rising inflection of happiness in her voice. "I've been all wrong, wrong about Elsie's father, but even more wrong about Elsie! She has proved that by running away with her father. The blessed darling! The poor lamb!"

Kate felt that she was on a merry-go-round of surprises. "You are glad she has run away?"

"How can I be anything but rejoiced!"

Kate turned a little cold at that. "And you won't try to stop them?" she asked.

"No, no need. Nick says he will give me their address as soon as they have one. Then I shall go to them, wherever it is. I will bring them back. Kate, she must *adore* her father! And all the while, just because she kept the agreement not to speak of him, I thought her indifferent to his sufferings, and unnatural. Why, from this, she must have suffered more than he." Miss Frazier tapped the folded letter with her lorgnette. "He says that when he looked in at your party and saw Elsie so beautifully gowned, and having such a good time, his heart failed him; he decided that he must not take her away from all this. But Elsie herself made him see that she would never be happy anywhere but with him no matter how poor they were. It was Elsie who insisted on this harebrained scheme of running away! Elsie, who I thought hadn't a grain of spirit or affection! Why, I'm just turned topsy-turvy by it all! Bless that poor child! And Nick wrote 'The King of the Fairies.' I ought to have guessed that instantly. Bless him, I say, too, the poor, abused, misguided poet. Do you remember St. Francis? You know he, too——"

But Miss Frazier broke off in her song of praise.

"You poor child, you," she cried, meaning Kate. "This must all be a mystery. We'll wait till your mother is here. Then we can talk it all over." She hugged Kate as she spoke, much as though she herself were a young girl in the most exuberant of spirits.

"I shall wear my black lace," she said, pushing Kate laughingly away from her. "We must be gorgeous for your mother. Hurry into your pink organdie. Why, she may be at the door this minute."

Thus freed, Kate flew to Elsie. Elsie was waiting, almost ill with anxiety. "Did you manage it?" she asked.

"No. And she has read the letter. But she is *glad*, Elsie. There's just to be no trouble about your getting away with your father at all."

"Didn't I tell you!" Elsie exclaimed. "It's just as I knew. She is glad to be rid of me."

"We must plan quickly, though. How will you get out? It's so dark now you can't see the orchard well at all. Let's plan."

Bertha was there, flushed and nervous. That morning Elsie had found it necessary to confide the secret of her father's being in the orchard house to Bertha, if he was to have any breakfast or lunch that day at all. They had let the food supply get very low, she and her father, because, until he had looked in at the party, they had expected to fly last night. Bertha was horrified at finding herself part of the intrigue, but there was no help for it since Elsie could always "Wind her around her little finger." Now, the almost distracted maid promised to stand by Elsie until the end. It would be the end for her as well as Elsie, for she would certainly lose her place to-morrow, and her character with it. For if Miss Frazier did not become aware for herself that Bertha had taken food to Nick in the orchard house this morning, and protected Elsie from the betrayal of her plans, Bertha meant to confess these things to her.

The three in conclave now decided that Elsie should go, after Kate and Miss Frazier were in the drawing-room, to the window seat on the stair landing. There she could conceal herself behind the curtains with her suitcase until Kate came out into the hall below, on some pretext to be found by her, and whistled softly. The whistle would mean that Katherine had come in and that Elsie could slip away to the orchard house unobserved.

All this was rather fun for Kate except for the sorry fact that when it was over she would have lost a comrade. To help stage a real runaway—well, it doesn't happen every day that one may be so at the centre of exciting events.

With Bertha's help Kate was dashing into her organdie while Elsie stood in a balcony window watching the orchard. Elsie had come in to be near Kate until the very last minute. But when a knock suddenly sounded on Kate's door Elsie wisely whisked away into her own room.

"Come," Kate called in a tremulous voice. Was it her mother? No, it was Aunt Katherine, and very fortunate it was that Elsie had been spry in her whisking.

"I see you are dressed," Miss Frazier said. "Come down, with me, then, and we will be together in the drawing-room when your mother arrives. I have ordered dinner delayed for her."

Kate thought quickly. "Just a minute," she said. "There's something in Elsie's room I need. Will you wait?"

Kate closed the door behind her as though by accident. But Elsie was not in the room. Kate looked all around but it was quite empty. The vanishing comrade had vanished, physically this time. There was the closet door. Was she hiding there? Yes, Kate heard a stir and saw dimly through the hanging dresses—expensive dresses given Elsie by Aunt Katherine, which she was not taking with her—Elsie herself squeezed back against the farthest wall. Kate closed the closet door behind her and groped her way across the dark closet. "It's I, Kate," she whispered loudly.

The girls touched hands in the dark. They hugged and kissed each other, mostly on noses and ears, but no matter; it was a grief-stricken parting. "Good-bye, good-bye," they whispered, and Kate said, "Write to me from California." But she must hurry back before it came into Miss Frazier's head to follow her in here with the idea of going through Elsie's door into the hall. She ran back to her own room and in her anxiety created the impression of a small cyclone appearing.

Miss Frazier looked with some surprise on the violence of her return. Then her eyes softened. Kate had not given thought to drying her tears. "You mustn't take it like this," Aunt Katherine said, putting her arm through Kate's as they went down the passageways together toward the big upper hall. "Elsie is happier than she has been in a very long time; she is off with one of the most satisfying companions in the world. Nick will take good care of her, infinitely better care than was ever taken here by me, for he *knows her mind.* And oh, Kate, we mustn't let your mother run away with you, too. Then I *should* be alone! You won't be without companionship. There are the Dentons just next door, and plenty of others who will be wanting to know you now."

"But they aren't Elsie," Kate responded, shamelessly using her handkerchief, as the tears would keep flooding.

CHAPTER XXI
LIKE THE STARS

Miss Frazier was too excitedly nervous to take up a book or knitting when they were in the drawing-room. She wandered about, looking at the pictures on the walls, picking up magazines from tables to stare at them vacantly and replace them again, changing the arrangements of flowers, and all the time she was waiting for the sound of the opening front door and Katherine's step in the hall. Kate was listening, too, but not in that direction. She expected her mother to come through the gardens and in at one of the French doors, closed now, with the rain beating against them. Kate was so absorbed with the consciousness of Elsie waiting up on the stair landing for her chance to escape that she forgot her mother had no umbrella and that she might be waiting in the orchard house until this particular shower passed. She merely wondered what was keeping her all this time, and what would happen when she and Aunt Katherine met. Aunt Katherine would certainly be surprised when she caught sight of the expected traveller through the glass doors on the terrace. There would be questions and explanations about that. Nick would have warned Katherine, of course, not to give away the secret of his being there; but then what *would* she give as her explanation to Aunt Katherine?

Would she be expecting to find Aunt Katherine here at all, though? Wouldn't Nick have acquainted her with the fact of Aunt Katherine's supposed absence? In that case Katherine, unprepared, would be hard put to it to give any excuse for entering through the gardens from the back, rather than by the front door, ushered in by Isadora. Kate was on tenter-hooks. She felt that it was she herself who had caused the muddle. But what could she have done differently? If she had told Aunt Katherine, up in her room, that Katherine was here already, only out in the orchard house, Aunt Katherine would certainly have gone straight out there, and then what would have happened to Nick and Elsie?

It was a bad ten minutes for Kate. She sat with a book open before her— what book she never knew—her eyes glued to the page, her ears cocked for a sound beyond the glass doors. Aunt Katherine stopped before her in her wanderings once or twice, about to speak, but she had too much respect for a reader to break into such obvious absorption as was Kate's.

Now Miss Frazier was standing looking through the glass of one of the doors into the rain-swept garden. Kate was seized with an idea. She must run up to Elsie in the window seat—she must manage it without her aunt's noticing, now—and send Elsie to the orchard house to warn those two that Miss Frazier had returned. After that, responsibility would be theirs. They might fix up some scheme among them. Kate rose, softly, and took a step toward the hall. But she was halted by an exclamation from Aunt Katherine.

Miss Frazier had not turned; she was still looking out through the glass. Kate, looking, too, saw two figures just at the edge of the orchard. It was her mother and Nick. Well, she could do nothing now. They certainly were counting on Aunt Katherine's absence, for they were coming toward the house. They were running toward the house, "between the drops," dashing like school children. They were holding hands, and Nick was always a step ahead, rather dragging Katherine. Oh, why hadn't Kate thought about an umbrella! They were laughing! Kate heard their laughter through the glass. So did Aunt Katherine. Her face, taken at that moment, would have made a perfect mask to personify Surprise.

She opened the doors, and Katherine and Nick blew through them like two drenched leaves. The rain had blurred the glass, and the running pair had thought it was Kate standing there watching them and letting them in. When they saw that it was Aunt Katherine they stood and simply *stared*, with almost no expression, still gripping each other's hands.

Miss Frazier's first words were unexpected ones. "Where is Elsie?" she asked Nick. That was all, just "Where is Elsie?" as though that, for the instant, was the thing of prime importance to her. It was Kate who could answer, though. Timidly she said, "Elsie's up on the stair landing."

"Well, that's all right, then. I thought she might be in search of a father in the South Station or some place. I thought, Nick, you two, you and Elsie, had run away."

Nick said, "We were going to. It is Katherine who has stopped us at the very minute." He still held Katherine's hand. Now he turned and looked at her. She looked back at him. Both Aunt Katherine and Kate, seeing what passed between their eyes, gasped. But it forewarned them, and Katherine's words when she spoke were only an echo of what they had seen.

"Nick and I are getting married, Aunt Katherine. We didn't know you were here, or we wouldn't have burst in like this. We had come to tell our children. Won't you get Elsie, Kate?"

"You and Nick marrying? So at last you've come to your senses!" That was Aunt Katherine.

"Yes. And oh, Aunt Katherine, she knows everything about me, and still she wants to."

"Well, of course she knows everything about you. I fancy *that's* had publicity enough. But if this is the way you feel, Katherine, why didn't you write me one word when Nick got himself into trouble? Or since? Your silence has been as cruel as any part of it all. It said plainer than words, 'Like Mrs. Van Vorst-Smith, I expected this sort of thing.'"

"Why, Aunt Katherine! How can you? If I had known Nick was in prison, that something so terrible had happened, I should have written you right away. No, I should have come. Trouble like that would have brought us all together. But how could I know, when nobody told me?" Katherine's beautiful eyes were like a grieved, accusing child's. "And what hard-shelled little creatures we are! Why couldn't my *soul* have told me?"

"Don't talk about your soul telling you." Aunt Katherine was brusque. "What about your eyes? Don't you ever read the papers?"

Katherine dropped her head. She had probably often dropped it so in the past before her aunt. "You know," she said, softly apologetic, "I never did read the papers as you do, Aunt Katherine, or keep up with current events."

Aunt Katherine laughed. It was a nice laugh. Kate visualized their brook in Ashland, when the ice was dissolving under the sun in the spring. (Yes, she did. It may seem a strange time for her mind to wander so far, but the fact remains. She saw the brook that zigzagged through the meadows back of their barn-house, as she had seen it last spring, its edges still frosted with ice, but down the centre the clear, laughing water coursing.)

"Well, the news of Nick would hardly come under 'current events'," Aunt Katherine was saying. "But I do remember now that you never did take a proper interest in the papers. It never entered my head, though, that you wouldn't have learned of this from a dozen sources."

Kate had been backing away toward the door, meaning to go for Elsie. But there was no need. Elsie had heard her father's voice the minute he had come into the drawing-room. She had stolen down into the room now, and gripped Kate's hand. Together the two girls moved back toward the three who were earnestly talking, still standing near the open door with the rain, all unobserved, discolouring the polished floor.

Aunt Katherine was asking Katherine another question. "Why didn't you take Nick seventeen years ago?" she asked. "You seem sure enough of yourself now. He wasn't good enough for you then. Is he good enough now after all that has happened?"

Again Katherine cried, "How can you!" But quickly she amended it. "Yes, you have a right. You know yourself, Aunt Katherine, what was the matter with me. It was pride of birth, blindness, love of luxury, Mrs. Van Vorst-Smith's head-shakings, a jumble of folly. You know perfectly what sort of a girl I was. But now I'm different. Now I'm nearer to being good enough for Nick."

"Love of luxury!" Miss Frazier picked on that. "You want me to believe your horrid description of yourself? If you loved luxury so much, why have you been living as you have all these years, accepting nothing of the luxuries I longed to give you?"

"But I tell you I changed. At twenty-two I was different from nineteen. I welcomed poverty then. When they told me that Kate and I had actually nothing to live on, I was delighted."

"So it has been by way of penance, your hard life since?"

"If you want to call it that. It's been fun, too."

"But not fun for me." Aunt Katherine's eyes filled with tears. For a person of Aunt Katherine's character to cry openly like that was as extraordinary a happening as though she had suddenly begun walking on her hands. Only Katherine dared speak to her or try to offer comfort. She put her arms around her shoulders, and led her to a chair. There she made her sit down, and knelt by her side, leaning her head against her arm, stroking her hand.

"Dear, dear, Aunt Katherine. Don't, don't," she besought. "We can't bear it. Oh, what have I done to you! What have we both done to you, Nick and I? Forgive us, Aunt Katherine. Love us again."

At that, even in the midst of her tears, Aunt Katherine laughed, and as before Kate remembered the brook. "Again!" Aunt Katherine exclaimed. "Did you think I had ever stopped loving either of you mad children?"

Nick nodded. "*I* have forfeited your affection right enough. I understand why you couldn't meet me, Aunt Katherine, two weeks ago when I asked you to. At least I understand now. I shouldn't have asked it. But how else were we to decide about Elsie?"

Aunt Katherine looked up at her adopted nephew, remembering. "But of course I did go to meet you," she said. "Did you think I wouldn't! I read the day, though, 'Thursday' instead of 'Tuesday.' It's not often I blunder so stupidly. Then I made frantic efforts to locate you. But you had vanished. There wasn't a trace. I set private detectives to work. To-day they took me all the way to Springfield on a wild-goose chase. They were sure they had located you there. Clever, those detectives!"

Aunt Katherine dried her eyes thoroughly as she spoke. She was scornful of her tears. "That excursion has tired me," she explained. "The disappointment of it. I was so downhearted. Then having you suddenly here again, right here at home, without warning, safe and happy—well, perhaps a sphinx would cry."

It was Nick's turn to kneel and rub his cheek against Aunt Katherine's shoulder. She lifted a hand and stroked his hair. Kate, too, got as close to her aunt as she could. Only Elsie stood aloof, for an instant not in any way part of the group. It was Aunt Katherine who beckoned her, and took her hand.

"Elsie," she said, "I have been thinking you hard and selfish because you kept my rule not to mention your father. I have wanted to speak with you of him, but every time I led up to it I thought you drew away. It seemed to me that you were suffering, not for him, but for your own wounded vanity. Now I understand better. Perhaps, in time, you will forgive me."

Then it was Elsie's turn to cry, and she did it so whole-heartedly that the family devoted its complete attention to calming her.

It was later that Miss Frazier exclaimed as though she had just remembered it: "So you two children are to be married, and Katherine become a Frazier again! I wonder what Oakdale will say to that turn of affairs!"

"If you really care what they say, Aunt Katherine"—Katherine spoke quickly—"need they know at all? Ashland society notes will hardly penetrate here. And you've had quite enough to bear."

"Don't think you could ever hide such a famous author as Nick has become, with only his first book, under a bushel for long, my dear. And as a matter of fact, quite apart from my joy that you are acting like a sane girl at last, and for once, I shall be proud to death of the marriage. I must call up the *Gazette* to-morrow, before ten. You remind me, Kate." As well as pride there was a gleam of battle from Aunt Katherine's eyes.

"And it really doesn't matter a bit what they do say, except for you, Aunt Katherine," Katherine offered. "There are four of us now, four in this family. Enough of us to stand together, I should think, and not ask much from society."

"Four? Five!" Kate left Elsie's side on the divan to perch on the arm of her great-aunt's chair. "Why, five of us are quite enough to start a colony and make our own society."

"Bless you, dear child, for counting me in," Miss Frazier said with sheerest gratitude.

"But of course, we all count you in, and there *are* five of us," Katherine cried, "only we don't want you to sacrifice too much." And that was the signal for a second close formation of happy people about Aunt Katherine's chair.

"Sacrifice! Why, all I want in the world is my family. Don't talk about sacrifice!"

It was much later that Aunt Katherine began wondering about dinner. What had become of it? Nick and Katherine had utterly forgotten that one does usually dine sometime before bedtime. They laughed at the suddenness of their return to earth.

"Ring the bell, Kate, and see if the servants are dead or asleep," Miss Frazier said.

But at that instant Effie appeared in the door. She had heard Miss Frazier's words. "Julia put dinner off an hour," she explained. "It's served now."

The "now," however, was almost lost in Katherine's sudden pounce upon the servant and her hearty handshake.

"Julia often takes a good deal upon herself," Miss Frazier observed, as linked with Katherine she led their little procession toward the dining-room.

And their first view of the table justified Aunt Katherine in this criticism of Julia. The polished surface of the cherished antique was hidden under an enormous damask cloth. But worse than that, the jade dish with its exquisite floating blossoms had given way to a huge, and to Miss Frazier's mind hideous, cut-glass punch-bowl full of roses, dozens and dozens of roses, pink, red, and yellow!

"Why, they have made it into a festival," Katherine cried, surveying the effect. "Smell those roses."

"See them, rather," Miss Frazier responded. "It's the servants. They must have known you both were here; and yes, there are two extra places set."

"It's Julia, the lamb!" Katherine declared. "Bless her dear heart. I saw her looking from the kitchen window as we ran in. I'd go and kiss her this second, but she wouldn't approve of that until after dinner. Julia's a lion for etiquette."

"Please be so considerate as not to begin spoiling the servants, Katherine."

Nick and Kate and Elsie looked at Aunt Katherine, surprised. But Katherine simply answered lightly, "It's they who spoil me." She accepted the tone of her aunt's command without dismay. She knew that the apparent sharpness had been only Aunt Katherine's old habit of criticism reasserting itself toward a beloved niece, who to her mind could never possibly be anything but the child she had "brought up." Katherine had begun to understand her aunt to-night for the first time, to see her in the "other light" that the King of the Fairies knew.

"You'd better excuse yourself to wash your hands and remove that odd-looking rain-soaked tam," Aunt Katherine picked on her again, the minute they were seated. "Use my bathroom, it's the nearest. And hurry right back, or this surprisingly sumptuous-looking soup that Julia has provided will get cold."

Katherine, obediently leaving the room, looked rather like a humble child, but Nick's eyes, as he stood, followed as though hers might have been the departure of an empress.

*   *   *   *   *   *   *   *

Late that night the doors between the girls' rooms blew shut in the wind that was clearing the air of storm and rain. Never mind about the doors, though; the spirit of Miss Frazier's rule rather than the letter was being kept to-night. For Kate and Elsie were curled up within whispering distance of each other on Kate's bed. Both were in dressing gowns; they were supposed to have been asleep for an hour past.

"I've never been abroad, or even anywhere out of New England," Kate was whispering. "You went with Aunt Katherine last summer. Will it be so wonderful as I expect?"

"We were only in England. And it will be a million times more wonderful than then, for we shall be together. Why, two weeks from now, sooner, we ought to be in Switzerland."

"And two weeks ago we had never heard of each other," Kate added.

"And one day ago," Elsie took it up, "if you had told me that I would spend the rest of the summer away from my father, travelling in Europe with you and Aunt Katherine, I would have said you were crazy."

"Oh, Elsie," Kate asked quickly, "I haven't said anything, but is that awfully hard for you, leaving them in Ashland, while we go so far away?"

"Not any more awful for me to leave my father than for you to leave your mother, I guess. Anyway, when *they* like the plan so much, we'd be funny daughters not to be pleased, too."

"You say 'My father, your mother'—Oh, Elsie, do you realize in just a day or two it will be 'our father and our mother'?"

Elsie nodded. "Yes, Kate," she said. "You have given me a mother and I have given you a father, and now we are a family. I feel, do you know, as though my heart might burst!"

"Don't let it," Kate warned quickly. "You'll need it strong for climbing the Alps! Imagine! Oh, how glorious it all is!"

"And when we come home again and live in that funny little barn-house of yours—I am thinking of that," Elsie whispered. "That will be better than travelling."

"The Hart boys are going to be simply flabbergasted," Kate said, remembering them. "They kept telling me to bring you home with me, but they never guessed you'd be my sister when you did come."

"But do you think they will want to have anything to do with me?" Elsie asked, diffidently.

"Why not, I should like to know?"

"Well, you see, that letter they wrote——"

Kate's face reddened. "What a creature I was! Of course, they will forget all about that now. Even if you weren't my sister and Mother's daughter, they'd like you awfully just the first second they saw you. They couldn't help it."

Before going to bed, finally, the girls put out the lights and went out on to Kate's flowery balcony to look at the clearing night. They stood close together, their arms about each other's shoulders, their dressing gowns billowing in the fresh wind. Elsie lifted her face up toward the sky. "It's going to be a fair day to-morrow," she affirmed. "See the stars!"

Kate's face was lifted, too. "Yes," she said. "Do you remember what the King of the Fairies told Hazel and her lover about the magic they had made their very own, how it's safer than the stars from troubling? Well, do you know, *as a family*, I think we are going to have a lot of that magic."

THE END

Milton Keynes UK
Ingram Content Group UK Ltd.
UKHW020828231024
450026UK00004B/456